CRYSTAL LEGENDS

Also by Moyra Caldecott

FICTION
Guardians of the Tall Stones:
The Tall Stones
The Temple of the Sun
Shadow on the Stones
The Silver Vortex

Weapons of the Wolfhound
The Eye of Callanish
The Lily and the Bull
The Tower and the Emerald
Etheldreda
Child of the Dark Star
Hatshepsut: Daughter of Amun
Akhenaten: Son of the Sun
Tutankhamun and the Daughter of Ra
The Ghost of Akhenaten
The Winged Man
The Waters of Sul
Adventures by Leaf Light and Other Stories

MYTHS AND LEGENDS
Crystal Legends
Three Celtic Tales
Women in Celtic Myth
Myths of the Sacred Tree
Mythical Journeys: Legendary Quests

POEMS
The Breathless Pause

AUTOBIOGRAPHY
Multi-dimensional Life

BIOGRAPHY
Oliver Z.S. Caldecott

CRYSTAL LEGENDS

by

Moyra Caldecott

Published by
Bladud Books

Moyra Caldecott has asserted her right under the Copyright,
Designs and Patents Act, 1988, to be identified as the Author of
this work

First published in 1990
by Aquarian Press

This edition published in 2007 by
Bladud Books, an imprint of
Mushroom Publishing, Bath, BA1 4EB, UK

Cover illustration by
Oliver Caldecott

ISBN 978-1-84319-326-5

Printed and Bound by
Lightning Source

CONTENTS

*The question is whether
awareness should itself
be made the object
of the search,
or instead gratefully
received as the fruit of
another quest altogether*

Stratford Caldecott, *In Search of the Miraculous*
(COMMUNIO, Summer 1989)

Introduction

There is a West African legend about a Box of Stories in the possession of the Sky God and the efforts of Anansi, the Spider, to buy it from him. The price he was set was to bring certain beings to the Lord of the Sky: Onini, the python; Osebo, the leopard; Moboro, the hornet; and Mmoatia, "the fairy that none can see".

Full of determination but not knowing which way to turn to fulfil these impossible tasks, he turned to his wife. When he mentioned the python she said he should use a piece of vine. "Say no more," he cried, and rushed off into the jungle to cut a long piece of vine. Onini, the python, lying somnolently on a huge branch, overheard him saying "It is larger than he is. No, it is shorter. No, it is longer..." Within minutes he had uncoiled from the tree and was asking Anansi what he was doing. The Spider claimed that he was trying to settle an argument with his wife as to whether this piece of vine was longer or shorter than Onini, the python, and persuaded Onini to lie down on the riverbank to be measured. As soon as he did so, of course, the vine was wound tightly around him and he was taken to the Lord of the Sky.

With similar guile, and each time at the suggestion of his wife, Anansi captured the other three creatures. Osebo, the leopard, fell into a deep hole dug by Anansi and was "rescued" by tying himself to the end of a vine which Anansi then used to haul him up before the Lord of the Sky. The hornet was persuaded it was raining and that the only way to keep dry was to climb into Anansi's hollow calabash. As soon as he was inside, of course, Anansi slammed shut the lid. The fairy was more difficult, but even she was tricked by a doll who sat in the forest with a lap full of yams. Thinking the yams were an offering for her the fairy reached out for them and instantly stuck fast on the thick honey Anansi had taken care to spread over them.

At last Anansi had earned the price of the Box of Stories. Excitedly he returned home and set it down in the middle of his village. He called everyone to gather round and told them the story of how he had come by this beautiful carved box. They listened to every word, sighing with relief as each being was captured and Anansi was nearer and nearer to obtaining the precious box.

It was now time to open the box. Everyone leaned forward. All eyes were on it. Anansi opened it carefully, slowly... but no sooner was the lid prized off than the stories sprang out and began flying everywhere. Anansi and his friends rushed and jumped and caught as many as they could – but many escaped and flew far away into the world to be caught by others.

I have been reaching out and trying to catch some of the stories about crystals in the world, and this book is the result.

A story needs the latent power of the python, the capacity to coil and uncoil and always stay alert and watchful; the strength and swiftness of the leopard to leap to the point after the slow coiling and uncoiling of the plot; the capacity to sting like a hornet no matter how small and short. But without the "fairy" it will not become one of the great stories of the world. It will not be one of the ones that escaped from the sacred box bought from the King of the Sky. It must have the qualities of a fairy – otherworldly qualities – meanings that creep up on you unseen to affect your whole perception of life. To catch a fairy with the honey of a story suggests very well how the story captures better than any other form of human expression – the inexpressible.

The crystals and precious stones that occur in the stories I have chosen are potent symbols. "Mysticism lives by symbols, the only mental representation by which the Absolute can enter our relative experience," writes F. Rècéjac, and again: "Symbolical signs have the same effect as direct perceptions; as soon as they have been 'seen' within, their psychic action takes hold of the feeling and fills the consciousness with a crowd of images and emotions which are attracted by the force of analogy."

I hope I have not killed the stories I have summarized here by trying to comment on what they might mean. Stories should he told or read and enjoyed, their magic working deep in the subconscious or high in the supraconscious, with our ordinary consciousness, as it were, in temporary suspension. I do not intend my commentaries to be analysis, but rather personal musings which I trust will set the reader off on a journey of exploration of his or her own.

Anansi worked hard to win the Box of Stories and that was only fair – because stories are not the valueless trifles some people think. They are among the greatest treasures of the world.

Through the ages certain stories have evolved that are so universal in their appeal and so exactly fit human experience at the deepest level that they help us to cope with what would otherwise be the chaotic and terrifying impact of the outside world.

When scientific and rational knowledge broke away from intuitive and instinctive knowledge these stories – these myths and legends – were dismissed as nonsense and relegated to children. In the households of very rational people, even children were denied their aid. Lately, having discovered that the route these scientists and rationalists insisted we take has led us into a horrifying impasse, and following such great thinkers as Jung, we are trying to reinstate the ancient myths, the healing stories, to their rightful place complementing and illuminating the other types of knowledge available to us.

Story is a natural need, and if we deny ourselves its benefits we may well suffer all kinds of maladies. We all know how our hearts beat faster when we think we hear a burglar in our house, whether there is one there or not. We hear an unfamiliar sound, and we tell ourselves a story of being robbed and murdered. Our body instantly reacts in all kinds of unpleasant and very physical ways. By the same token, faced by the frightening and immense forces of the universe we can calm ourselves, comfort and encourage ourselves, with a well-chosen myth.

Story can both kill and heal, as any witch doctor, faith healer, or psychologist knows.

The depth psychologist James Hillman once said in an article for *Parabola*, the American journal dedicated to Myth and the Quest for Meaning: "From my perspective I see that those who have a connection with story are in better shape and have a better prognosis than those to whom story must he introduced... To have 'story-awareness' is *per se* psychologically therapeutic. It is good for the soul." He also said: "The main body of Biblical and Classical tales directs fantasy into organized, deeply life-giving psychological patterns; these stories present the archetypal modes of experiencing."

There is no doubt in my mind that a well tried story, a myth, a legend, rich in inner meaning, teaches and heals. The two processes work together to make the recipient "whole". It is often the fragmentation of consciousness – the warring of different parts of the consciousness – that makes for ill health. One's "heart" tells one that existence has meaning and purpose. One's "brain" denies it. The story builds a bridge between the two contraries, enabling each to come to terms with the other – each to see the truth in the other.

"Woe to the sinners who look upon the Torah as simply tales pertaining to things of the world, seeing thus only the outer garments," says the *Zohar*. "But the righteous whose gaze penetrates to the very Torah, happy are they. Just as wine must be in a jar to keep, so the Torah must be contained in an outer garment. That garment is made up of the tales and stories; but we, we are bound to penetrate beyond."

In this book I'm trying to penetrate beyond. I know I haven't arrived, but I hope at least I've suggested a few paths to take. As Deena Metzeger said in his article "Circle of Stories": "Stories go in circles. They don't go in straight lines. So it helps if you listen in circles because there are stories inside stories and stories between stories and finding your way through them is as easy and as hard as finding your way home. And part of finding is getting lost. If you're lost, you really start to look around and listen." Later he says: "Stories have many feet and travel several roads at once to the wisdom of the heart..."

* * * *

This is a book about the stories, the myths and legends, that use crystals and precious and semi-precious stones as potent and powerful symbols.

Crystals and gemstones have fascinated human beings since Neolithic times, and no doubt will continue to do so until the end. They endure when the bones of those whom they adorned have turned to dust, and it is usually they and only they that give us knowledge of the people who lived in ancient times. They speak a universal language capable of being interpreted by any people, any age. Scythians, Egyptians, Iranians, Indians, Celts, Romans – all wore them in life and tried to take them with them in death. Even Christians, who don't believe the dead person will need the accoutrements of this life in the next, hesitate to part a woman from her wedding or engagement ring when she is laid in the earth – though everything else is stripped away.

We return to dust, but the gem on our finger still quietly gleams through the buried centuries and emerges at last, turned up by the plough or the probing trowel of the archaeologist to be displayed in a museum where people in their thousands gaze at it and thrill to the sense of continuity, of ancient, rooted mystery. The real value of the gem cannot be measured in currency, but in the sense it gives us of wonder that the earth can produce such extraordinary and secret beauty... that hidden from us, but capable of being discovered, is something more than the mundane dirt and rubble of our lives... that such orderly and precious form might indicate conscious design. In our moments of terror in a world that appears to release random and wanton horrors on us from time to time, such an indication brings hope and comfort.

Crystals have fascinated me all my life and I have been collecting them for more than half a century. Most of that time I had no idea why I did so except that they were beautiful and they made me feel happy, and comforted me in moments of despair. If I had tried to explain why I turned to them in this way, I would have said that it was because they reminded me that I was on a magnificent planet hurtling through space, conceived in Mystery and born into splendour. I would stand on the tarmac of a big city with the traffic roaring by, or in an underground train squashed against my fellow human beings, half suffocated, mind assaulted by the anxious jabbering thoughts of those around me, and touch the crystal in my pocket, instantly experiencing relief. What I could see around me was not, after all, all there was to life on earth. It was as though the secret energy contained in that harmonious and beautiful natural form helped to reorientate all the tangled threads of my disordered mind, so that they lay calmly, in a neat but vibrant pattern.

There is today a growing movement of people seeking out the ancient crystal lore. Crystal-wisdom workshops and healing centres have proliferated. Shops selling crystals are everywhere, and where before only the fey and unworldly would wear a crystal against their hearts, now the hard-headed businessman goes into board meetings believing that the crystal in his pocket or hidden under his shirt will help him clinch a deal.

As always with the human race some people go too far. They take up an idea and run with it so enthusiastically that they have long passed the finishing line before they realize that the race is over and the other contestants are going home. Some people claim too much for crystals, and I'm afraid that, because they do so, the general public will turn against this ancient and honourable wisdom, throwing, once again, "the baby out with the bathwater". Crystals do have a certain power and a very real energy. A part of it may be the physical response of the vibrationary rate of our own bodies to the vibrationary rate of the crystal, but more than that I believe it is the expectation we have of the crystal, an expectation built up over centuries, even millennia, now deep in our collective subconscious and ready to be used.

Just to take quartz crystal for a moment: in ancient pre-Celtic Britain white quartz crystal was not only of prime importance in the choosing of the tall stones for the sacred circles, but was used extensively in the burials and initiations. Important burial mounds and initiation chambers (for example New Grange in Ireland) were often covered entirely with quartz, and many skeletons in barrow burials have been found with a quartz crystal beside them or clutched in their bony hands.

The tall stones in the prehistoric stone circles and single standing stones around the world have predominantly a very high quartz content, most of them specifically chosen not only for the crystalline nature of the rock itself, but for the prominent intrusions of quartz veining in them. At Duloe in Cornwall, England, near Looe, there is a circle in a farmer's field constructed entirely of pure white quartz. Every stone (some of them ten feet tall) is of pure white quartz! Imagine it in its full glory in the ancient days (before pollution) with a full moon shining down upon it.

The universality of the use of quartz for magical or esoteric purposes was brought home to me one Christmas when my son and daughter-in-law, then living in Sarawak (North Borneo), gave me a present of a quartz crystal attached to a thong that had been worn by one of the local Penan people, the hunter-gatherers of the rain forest. I put it beside the quartz crystal I was already wearing around my neck, bought at a "New Age" festival in Britain. Crystals as talismans have been with us since cave-dwelling times and no doubt will be with us when we are living on Mars.

In his excellent book on shamanism, Mircea Eliade explains how shamans use crystals. The people of the Semang tribe on the Malay Peninsula believe that at the initiation of their shaman or medicine man, he is given quartz crystals by the celestial spirits – which he subsequently uses for healing. The spirits abide in the crystals and with their help the medicine man "sees in the crystals the disease that afflicts the patient and the means of curing it".

The shaman of the Sea Dyaks or Iban of East Malaysia (Sarawak) has a box containing a collection of magical objects, the most important being quartz crystals, "the stones of light". With the help of these he discovers the patient's soul. "For here too, illness is a flight of the soul and the purpose of the seance is to discover it and restore it to its place in the body."

Druid crystal eggs were thought to be so charged with magic

that someone facing a lawsuit was put to death if he was found to have one on him, on the grounds that he had an unfair advantage.

In Australia and in South America tribes believe that the shaman is taken during his initiation to some sacred cave, or mountain, or into the sky, where he is symbolically cut open and given a new set of internal organs. The new set is of quartz crystal, which gives him his power as shaman. One becomes a fully initiated shaman when "one is stuffed with 'solidified light', that is, with quartz crystals".

In Mircea Eliade's *Shamanism* there is an account of how the aboriginal candidate and his initiatory masters enter a rock. Once inside, the blindfold is removed from the eyes of the candidate and he "finds himself in a place of light with rock crystals glittering from the walls. He is given several of these crystals and told how to use them." Whoever has seen a geode, or is lucky enough to have one in their possession, will respond to this with a special tingle of recognition. Whoever has read Mary Stewart's novel about Merlin, *The Crystal Cave*, will know that she is using a universal and very potent archetype.

Is the modern American myth in which Superman seeks his knowledge and his strength among the magnificent collection of crystals brought from his home planet, based on the ancient American myth mentioned by Eliade, in which "a young man climbing a shining mountain, becomes covered with rock crystals and immediately begins to fly'?

The transparency, the hint of inner light, the quality of being solid and yet almost invisible – all these things must surely make the crystal a natural symbol for spiritual matters in legends and myths.

The symbol is chosen because the qualities of the crystal lend themselves to the analogy, but it gains in power over the centuries as it is used time and again in the stories that form the thinking patterns of the human race.

It is my belief that the power of crystals to heal, to help in the development of our psychic faculties, to be used for divination and meditation, is due as much to the legends and myths the race has been brought up with, as to the inherent energy of the crystal itself.

I started this introduction by talking about the importance of Story because I am very anxious not to be misunderstood here. I don't mean that the crystal has no power of its own and that we only think it has because we have been told about it in legends. Both the story and the crystal have a power, an energy, that cannot accurately be measured in a laboratory (though some scientists are now beginning to try!), and that power, that energy, is subtly bound up with the power, the energy of the human spirit – another thing the scientists cannot measure.

When the bicycle tones up the muscles of the body, it is not the well-being of the bicycle that we are primarily concerned with, but the well-being of the body. The crystal and the story (and more specifically for the purposes of this book – the crystal in the story) tones up the faculties of the spirit. The crystal does help the businessman to make his deal and does heal the sufferer of an illness, because it puts him or her in a state of mind in which, in the one case, clear thinking and decisiveness is enhanced, and, in the other, calmness and relaxation. I believe the gentle subliminal action of the physical vibrations of the crystal would have very little effect if it wasn't augmented by a deep belief in its efficacy. And I hold that belief has strengthened in us because of the myths and legends that are so importantly woven into our subconscious race memory.

I have mentioned the crystal as a potent symbol in myth and legend triggering reactions in the various levels of the consciousness, but I haven't so far mentioned that most significant and most misunderstood and undervalued faculty of the human mind – the imagination. "It's only your imagination" is a phrase we all know, and have heard innumerable times. "Don't let your imagination run away with you..." "You are imagining it..." In each case the implication is that imagination is something silly and should he discouraged. I believe that without the imagination the human race would still be "in the trees". I believe the imagination is the thrusting edge of the human soul as it reaches up towards the Higher Realms, searching for its lost union with its Deity. It gives us wings, and lifts us from the clay. It gives us eyes and we see the invisible. If we do not have imagination we might as well resign ourselves to the dust, for there is nothing more we will be able to experience but the dust. Without imagination we kill our fellow man because we cannot imagine what it would be like to be him. Without imagination the scientist will measure and weigh and count, but will never bring us the great discovery, the Nobel-prize-winning breakthrough.

Myths and legends are produced by the imagination when it is functioning at its most serious and profound level. The body is a finely tuned, immensely complex and efficient instrument capable of experiencing much more than we commonly give it credit for – and one of its functions is at once to house the "growing point" of the soul, and to protect it from the damage it might suffer if it were exposed to too much transcendent experience too soon. The imagination tests out the ground beyond ourselves and allows us to explore the way ahead in imaginal symbolic form before we have to encounter it in reality. The imagination gives us myths and legends – those marvellous, subtle, complex vehicles of esoteric teaching to prepare us for our future. In seeking their meaning we are meant to find the meaning of ourselves.

Life is, as you well know, inexplicable. All the religions in the world, all the myths and legends in the world, all the scientific theories and mathematical formulae, laid end to end, cannot give us a totally satisfactory explanation. But the story teller can give us a glimpse, a fleeting flash, of something that makes us feel we understand so that we can live out our lives with direction and purpose instead of floundering blindly in the dust and wasting our potential.

Everyone finds his or her own story to help him or her go forward in hope. Over the years I have been building up a picture of how I see life drawn from what I consider to be the basic teachings of all the great religions ("the Perennial Philosophy" as Aldous Huxley called it) before they were set at each other's throats by misunderstandings and misrepresentations. How I see the mystery of life obviously influences my interpretation of the myths and legends in this book. You might have a very different world-view, and consequently interpret the stories very differently. This is all right. The very ambiguity of myth is its strength. Myth is a kind of mirror – we see what we are capable of seeing, what we want to see, and what we need to see. We see ourselves, but in greater depth than we would in an ordinary mirror.

Sources

"The Box of Stories", story retold by Paul Jordan-Smith from one he heard told by Jay O'Callahan, *Parabola: Myth and the Quest for Meaning*, Vol. IV, No. 4, November 1979, pp. 25-8.

E. Récéjac, Essays on "The Bases of Mystic Knowledge", quoted in *An Anthology of Mysticism and Mystical Philosophy*, compiled by W. Kingland (Methuen, 1927).

James Hillman, "A Note on Story", *Parabola, Myth and the Quest for Meaning*, Vol. IV, No. 4, November 1979.

The Zohar: The Book of Splendours, basic readings from the Kabbalah selected and edited by Gershom G. Scholem (Rider, 1977), p. 122.

Deena Metzeger, "Circle of Stories", *Parabola*, Vol. IV, No. 4, November 1979.

Mircea Eliade, *Shamanism: Archaic Techniques of Ecstasy* (Bollingen Series, Princeton University Press, 1964).

You will find the stories in this volume in many different forms and in many different places. I have quoted only the sources I have specifically and recently consulted for the writing of this book.

Chapter 1

The Championship of Ireland and the Crystal Bird

(Western Europe: Celtic)

Everyone knew that Bricriu was a troublemaker, and no one wanted to have anything to do with him. Nevertheless he managed to persuade the three greatest heroes of Ireland and all their friends, relatives, and companions to come together at his house for a feast by dint of promising them worse trouble if they refused. His unwilling guests finally agreed to come on condition that he himself was not present. He agreed – but built himself a chamber above the hall where he could observe all that went on.

Before the guests entered the hall, however, Bricriu, as host and provider of the meat and mead, greeted them. While doing so he managed to have a private word with each of the three greatest heroes, Cuchulain, Conall Cernach, and Laegaire Buadach, mentioning to each that when it was time to serve the meat he was to claim the champion's portion because he, and none other, was the greatest hero of Ireland. He further compounded the mischief by telling each of the three heroes' wives privately that she, wife of the greatest hero of Ireland, should enter the feast hall ahead of all the other women. He then retired to his private room to watch the fun.

The strife he caused between the three heroes and the three wives spilled over well beyond the feast and occupied the Irish for quite a while thereafter. Rather than have the three heroes destroy each other and all around them over the matter, they were persuaded to submit to tests of strength and courage set by neutral arbitrators.

Watched over and egged on by their excited supporters, the three performed prodigious feats. In every one Cuchulain outdid the others. They fought giants and magical Druid cats; they fought fearsome spectres and armies of fierce warriors; but no matter how clear it was that Cuchulain outstripped the others, Conall and Laegaire would not admit that he was champion. They claimed something was wrong with the test and that Cuchulain had won unfairly.

At one point the whole crowd arrived at Cruachan, the stronghold of Ailell and Maeve, king and queen of Connaught. They demanded that King Ailell name the greatest hero once and for all.

Ailell was worried and spoke to his wife, complaining that he was in a very difficult position, for if he named one hero over the others, the other two and all their rowdy companions would go berserk and destroy everything in sight.

Queen Maeve suggested a clever solution that would at least save their own property.

One by one she called the three heroes to a private audience. She told Laegaire Buadach that he should have the hero's portion at the great feast of Conchubar, the High King. All he had to do was to produce a token she would give him that would leave no doubt as to who she thought the champion was. She gave him a bronze chalice with a bird of silver at the bottom. To Conall she gave the same speech and a chalice of silver with a bird of red gold at the bottom. Lastly she called Cuchulain to her side and presented him with a chalice of red gold with a bird of precious crystal in the bottom.

All three and their entourage of supporters then set off for the stronghold of Conchubar, the High King. On the way the contention continued and many a dangerous and skilful feat was performed to try to prove which one was the greatest hero of them all.

At last, at the court of Conchubar, the welcome feast was set.

Laegaire produced his chalice of bronze and proudly showed the bird of white silver at the bottom, saying that it had been given by Ailell and Maeve as token that he was the greatest champion of Ireland.

Conall laughed and stood up brandishing his chalice of silver, with the bird of red gold in the bottom.

"This was given me by Ailell and Maeve," he cried, "Judge for yourselves how much more they valued me than Laegaire Buadach."

Then Cuchulain strode across the room and slapped his chalice down in front of Conchubar.

Smiling, the king raised it above his head so that all could see the glowing vessel of red gold and, inside, the bird of precious crystal.

"Cheat!" Conall and Laegaire shouted. "He bribed them for the better cup."

Conchubar raised his strong right arm to prevent the fight that was about to break out and declared there would be one last and convincing test that would prove which one had the greatest courage and was therefore worthy to eat the champion's portion.

While they were waiting for the test to be devised an ugly, brutish man entered the hall and jeered at the heroes of Ireland, declaring that none of them would dare to meet his challenge.

"What challenge is that, you oaf?" Conall said, scarcely bothering to stop drinking long enough to say the words.

"To chop off my head," the man replied.

"That I will gladly do!" shouted Conall, laughing. "Just hand me your axe."

"The full challenge is that you cut off my head today, but I cut off your head tomorrow."

There was much shouting and jollity at this absurdity, and Conall took the axe from the man, swung it, and chopped off his head. He soon sobered up, however, when the man picked up his head and replaced it on his body, reclaimed his axe, and walked out of the hall.

The next day when he returned for the completion of the

challenge Conall was nowhere to be found. Laegaire was accosted by the oaf and, against his better judgement, shamed into accepting the challenge to prove that he was a greater hero than Conall.

He swung his axe. The man picked up his head and left the hall. The next day when he returned Laegaire was also missing.

The man then turned his attention to Cuchulain – and for honour's sake Cuchulain had to take up the challenge.

The next day when the man returned Cuchulain was waiting for him. He did not flinch once, though the man swung the axe three times, each time hitting his neck with the blunt edge of the weapon.

Then was the matter settled. The oaf revealed himself a master of Druid magic sent to test the three heroes.

To Cuchulain at last was given the champion's portion, and he quaffed his wine from the chalice of the crystal bird.

Comment

Bricriu the troublemaker represents that part of ourselves which, no matter how noble we are, tempts us to mischief, tests our credentials, shows up any flaws in our personalities. When I first began to read Celtic legends I was sometimes impatient with their unquestioning belief that the man who can kill the most people was accepted as the greatest hero. It was only when I began to put the lists of killings into the background as one does with something that is monotonous and boring that I began to notice other, more interesting things in the legends. True, the hero in the Irish heroic tales is still the man who can fight and kill more than anyone else, but in this story he is teased and mocked. He may have brawn, but has he got brain? How easily Bricriu stirs up the strife between them; how quickly they fall for his tricks. Violent and argumentative, they swagger around

Ireland, each refusing to accept the result of any of the tests, wreaking havoc wherever they go, egged on by their supporters.

The fact that there are three of them is interesting. Among the Celts three is the most potent and significant of numbers. There are three aspects of the Goddess; there are three crystal trees at the entrance to the Otherworld; there are three brothers or three sisters in almost every "fairy" story... It is said that the Irish took so readily to Christianity when the first missionaries came to them because they understood the concept of the Trinity so easily.

Here there are three heroes and it seems as though the problem of which one is the greatest will never he resolved. There is no doubt they are each capable of fighting and killing as well as the others, but the final test comes and only one of them can face *being* killed with unflinching courage. That is being killed not in the heat of battle but as a deliberate and sober fulfilment of a promise. The mysterious god who challenges the hero to cut off his head one day and then submit himself to having his own head severed the next, is a key concept in Celtic myth. In the Arthurian legends we have Gawain and the Green Knight. In this story a wild man enters the court of Conchubar, the High King. A "wild man'? Is he the nature god, the Green Knight, the earth itself? Is he asking for a blood sacrifice for the good of the earth? In ancient Celtic times the noblest of the heroes would offer himself as a sacrifice that the earth would burgeon in the spring. What we may be witnessing here is the choosing of the sacrifice – not an idle argument among the heroes as to which one is the greatest. Two of them back out at the last moment. Only Cuchulain is prepared to go the whole way, and bends his head in noble submission. Three times the ceremonial axe touches the back of his neck. He is given three chances to withdraw. He does not.

In a sense we already know which one is chosen when Cuchulain is given the chalice with the crystal bird. He has drawn "the long straw". The others have been honoured with silver and gold. They are heroic figures of the material world.

But the third chalice, the one that becomes the possession of the real and ultimate hero, carries the symbol of the spiritual world. In Celtic legend birds are almost always associated with the Otherworld. We have Rhiannon's magic birds in the Welsh legends; the two birds that swoop over the lake and entice Cuchulain away to Fand's beautiful spirit-world; the swans that so frequently prove to be spirit-beings...

The silver bird and the gold bird received by Conall and Laegaire in the cup of plenty, the chalice of life-giving liquid, are messengers too, but the crystal bird – the transparent one, the one that suggests the invisible and numinous realms of the Otherworld more readily – is the one that is given to Cuchulain.

Cuchulain is the god's choice and Cuchulain honours his calling with a good grace, all boasting and buffoonery past.

Sources

Early Irish Myths and Sagas, translated by Jeffrey Gantz (Penguin Classics, 1981).

Cuchulain of Muirthemne by Lady Gregory (Colin Smythe, Gerrards Cross, 1970).

Chapter 2

The Crystal Trees

(Western Europe: Celtic)

One day at Samhain, Cuchulain, Ulster's greatest champion, was beside a lake at Muirthemne with a group of companions when a flock of birds flew over the water. The women cried out that they wanted the feathers for their cloaks, and the men soon set about shooting them down. When the feathers were all distributed only one woman was left without, and that was Ethne Inguba, the mistress of Cuchulain. So disappointed was she that Cuchulain promised her he would find even better ones for her no matter what happened.

At that moment two birds came skimming low over the lake, so strange and beautiful that they gasped to see them. Cuchulain took aim with his sling at once and let fly. He missed and the birds wheeled and flew back across the lake. Embarrassed, for he was the surest shot in Ireland, Cuchulain loaded his sling again and was waiting when the pair darted back overhead.

"Leave them," cried Ethne, for she could see a fine chain of red gold between them and suspected that they were enchanted birds, birds of the Sidhe.

But Cuchulain let fly and once again missed them.

Now he was angry and red in the face, and the next time they appeared he flung his spear at them, dislodging a feather, but no more. They eluded him and flew across the lake and were not seen again.

Ethne tried to tell him it didn't matter, but he strode away from her angrily.

He came to rest at last against a standing stone, remote from all his friends. He sat down with his back against the granite, his head on his knees, ashamed that such a great marksman as he was should have made such a fool of himself.

Whether he was dreaming or not he could not tell, but it seemed to him at that point that two young women stood before him. They stared at him a moment and then one of them struck him with a rod. When she had done, the other did the same. They went on thus, alternately striking him, for some time. Both were smiling.

When they left him he was slumped against the stone in a daze.

His companions found him like that and took him to Ethne's home. He would say nothing to them and lay in bed with his face to the wall for a whole year. They were at their wits' end to know how to rouse him.

A year from the day the wasting sickness started, Cuchulain received a mysterious visitor. One of the Tuatha de Danaan appeared at his bedside and called him to come with him. Then he disappeared.

Cuchulain, sighing deeply, at last told his companions what had happened the year before. Conchubar the High King told him that he must return to the same stone where he had encountered the women and see if it were not possible to resolve the matter where it had started.

To the standing stone he went on the high day of the feast of Samhain when the gates between the worlds lie open.

It was not long before one of the women who had beaten him appeared.

"What do you want of me?" he asked.

"My sister Fand has fallen in love with you," she said. "Come with me and I will take you to her."

Cuchulain did not feel inclined to do so.

Seeing that, she continued: "I have a message from my husband."

"Who is your husband?" he asked suspiciously.

"He is Labraid of the Quick Sword," she replied, "and he offers you anything you might wish for if you will come and lend him your warrior strength against his enemies for one day."

"I am weak and ill," Cuchulain said. "I cannot fight."

"You will be healed."

Still Cuchulain hesitated, and he returned to his companions without giving the woman the answer she sought.

He sent Laeg, his charioteer, to tell Emer his wife all that had happened to him, and she came to him and roundly berated his companions for not telling her before what shape he was in, nor for helping him when he needed help. She then turned to him and roused him to his feet, demanding that he face whatever it was that was required of him like the champion he was supposed to be.

Cuchulain returned to the standing stone and once again met the young woman of the Sidhe. Once again she pleaded with him to come to the aid of her husband and her sister Fand,

This time he agreed to do so, but sent his charioteer Laeg with her to make sure that everything was as she had said.

Laeg brought back a glowing report of the land of the Sidhe, the island at the centre of the lake, the woman more beautiful than any other who pined for him, the hero of the Quick Sword who needed his help.

Cuchulain agreed at last to go himself.

He was taken across the lake in a fine and shining boat, and there on the island of the Sidhe passed through the eastern gate beside which grew three trees of crystal, melodious with birdsong.

Labraid told him the task he had to perform and he was led to the place of battle. There in a magical mist he fought with all his old skill and strength an enemy he could not see. Victorious at last, he was taken to Fand's bed and, forgetful of everything that had passed or was passing in the world of the mortals, made love to her.

He lived with her for a long time by earth measure, but aged not a day. It might be that he would have been with her yet, had not he felt the stirring of a memory one day, a longing for the old rough ways of the earth, and the pain in his eyes showed her that she could not keep a mortal man forever in her shining land when he was not ready for it.

They agreed that he should pass once again between the crystal trees and return to Ulster. She would follow him there and they would continue to be lovers in his world as they had been in hers.

But trees of wood and leaf change with the seasons, unlike the crystal trees of the Shining Lands, and when summer changed to autumn Cuchulain was caught between his love for the changing moods of the physical world and the changeless beauty of the Otherworld. He was confused, torn between the two women Emer, his earth-wife, and Fand, the spirit-woman. The two women faced each other. At last, for love of him, Fand sadly gave him up and gently withdrew back between the crystal trees.

Comment

The eastern entrance to the beautiful land of the Sidhe, the mysterious Otherworld where Cuchulain lives in bliss with Fand and does not age, is between trees of crystal.

In the Book of Revelation the heavenly city, standing in the glory of God, shines with a light "like unto a stone most precious – clear as crystal" (21: V. 10, 11). "And he shewed me a pure river of water of life, clear as crystal, proceeding out of the throne of God and of the Lamb. In the midst of the street of it, and either side of the river, was there the tree of life, which bare twelve manner of fruits, and yielded her fruit every month: and the leaves of the tree were for the healing of the nations... Blessed are they that do his commandments, that they may have right to the tree of life, and may enter in through the gates into the city" (22: 1, 2, 14).

Although St John does not say the trees in the heavenly Jerusalem are made of crystal, the crystal imagery is so closely associated with them that I have always seen them as crystal in my mind's eye, the image strengthened by so many other traditions. In the Islamic Paradise there is a tree covered with rubies, emeralds, and sapphires. In the ancient Egyptian Book of the Dead, spells 109 and 144 refer to the two trees of turquoise between which Ra, the sun-god, goes forth.

Everywhere one looks, in ancient legend or ancient sacred sites, crystal plays a major role as symbol for the passage between the worlds, between the mundane and the divine, between the material and the spiritual.

In the Celtic story of Cuchulain and the crystal trees the combination of the words "east" which represents sunrise and renewal, "trees' which remind us of the Tree of Life and the Tree of Knowledge, and "crystal" which suggests that we may see through the natural to the supernatural, produces a powerful and evocative image. Cuchulain is no longer in the ordinary world. He has entered a different reality – a reality that is eternally present and yet normally unnoticed by us. At the entrance to it are the crystal trees.

But he has taken a long time to reach this point of entering the Otherworld. The process started when he tried to shoot down the magical messengers from the Sidhe, the two beautiful birds linked by a golden chain swooping low over the lake. He had a glimpse of Otherworld reality, but was so much embedded in the material world that all he could think of was how to destroy what he saw and use it for the physical adornment of his mistress. He saw no other meaning in the experience. When he couldn't shoot them down, he was chagrined and shamed. His pride was hurt. For the first time his physical prowess (which was considerable) was of no use to him. He became depressed and sick. He could see no other way of living but by his physical skills, and he couldn't understand the message the birds were trying to bring him.

He sinks down in despair with his back to a standing stone – a place of great mystic potency. It is Samhain – that time of year when the Celts believed the gate between the worlds was open and it was easy to pass through from one to the other.

The two young women of the Sidhe who had appeared to

him first as birds, beat him. He suffers. His human pride is reduced to nothing. He doesn't know how to live without it. He retreats to his bed and turns his face to the wall.

A year later to the day, at Samhain, another messenger appears to him. For the first time Cuchulain tells his companions something of what had happened to him. No one understands the implications, but he is advised by the High King (a high priest?) to return to the standing stone and at least try to find out what it is all about.

He does so, and the call to the Otherworld is delivered clearly. The spirit-woman asks for his warrior strength to help her husband against his enemies. Cuchulain had lost his physical warrior strength when he entered the period of questioning and bewilderment that precedes acceptance of spiritual values. Warrior strength is the only kind of strength he understands, so the spirit uses that image to entice him, but the battle she wants him to fight for her husband is very different from the battle he is likely to fight on earth. When he eventually fights he fights "in a mist" an enemy he cannot see.

But at this point Cuchulain is still too fond of the world he knows, and does not dare to leave it no matter what the enticement is. Emer, his wife, his strong and intelligent mate, seeing that the life he is living now is no life at all, rouses him to face up to whatever challenge awaits him. Throughout the Cuchulain stories he meets challenge after challenge and does daring deeds beyond belief. He is no coward. This is the first one he has shirked, and he shirks it only because it is so much beyond his understanding. He clings, like most of us, to what he knows, fearing what he does not know.

At last, stung by her words, he goes back to the standing stone. But even so he hesitates: he sends his charioteer in his place – twice. Only at the third call does he go himself.

He passes between the crystal trees, he conquers himself believing he is conquering the enemy of the king. He unites with Fand, his Higher Self, and is blissfully happy for a while.

But the pull of the ordinary world is still too strong for him. He tries to have the best of both worlds by taking Fand back with him to his. But the ordinary world wins and Fand withdraws.

It is interesting that when Cuchulain is eventually slain in battle he chooses to die with his back against the standing stone. In death he enters the world he was unready to accept before. But that is in another story.

Sources

Early Irish Myths and Sagas, translated by Jeffrey Gantz (Penguin Classics, 1981).

Cuchulain of Muirthemne by Lady Gregory (Colin Smythe, Gerrards Cross, 1970).

Chapter 3

The Crystal Ball

(Western Europe)

A sorceress had three sons, and as they grew one by one to maturity she began to fear that they would outstrip her in the magical arts by stealing her secrets.

When she thought the first one had grown old enough to be a danger to her, she turned him into an eagle and sent him to circle the sky day after day. He made his home at the top of a mountain and lived as eagles lived. But once a day, for two hours, he reverted to his former shape and was aware of what had happened to him and sorrowed for it. But he was too far from home to do anything about it.

When she thought the second son was old enough to outwit her she turned him into a whale, and he circled the great oceans, crying with a whale's voice to the other whales that rode the wild water far, far from his home. He too was allowed two hours a day in human form, but was too far from home to do anything about it.

When the sorceress was in her secret room considering whether she should turn her third and youngest son into a wolf or a bear, he slipped away and fled, anxious that what had happened to his brothers would not happen to him.

In his wanderings he heard about a princess kept prisoner in the Castle of the Golden Sun by an enchanter, and determined to release her. He was warned that the task was difficult and dangerous and that twenty-three young men had already attempted it and each one had died in agony. Only one more attempt was to be allowed – after that the princess could never be rescued. But nothing would deter him. He was sure he would succeed where others had failed.

The first difficulty he encountered was that he couldn't find the Castle of the Golden Sun. He journeyed in every direction and followed many different instructions, but he seemed to be no nearer his destination.

One day he found himself lost in a deep, dark forest, and no matter which way he chose to walk he never seemed to get to the end of it. When he was almost in despair he came upon two giants in a clearing fighting over a hat. When they saw him they asked him to arbitrate between them.

"It's ridiculous to fight over a hat!" he said.

"But this is not just any old hat," they said. "It is a wishing hat. Anyone wearing the hat can wish to be anywhere in the world and in an instant find himself there."

"I'll tell you what we'll do," he said. "Give me the hat and I'll walk away. When I call, you race towards me and the first one to reach me has the hat."

They agreed to this at once because, although they were so huge, they were not very bright.

The young man put the hat on and walked away from the giants.

While he was walking he wished he could find the Castle of the Golden Sun, and instantly he was on a high mountain at the gate of the castle.

He entered it and began to look for the princess. Room after room proved to be empty, but in the very last one left to try, he found her.

She was not young and beautiful as he had expected, but shrivelled and dark and ugly. He couldn't help an exclamation of surprise, and, seeing his disappointment, she explained that the form he thought he saw before him was an illusion.

"Look at my reflection in this mirror," she said. "The mirror cannot be deceived. There you will see me as I really am."

He held up the mirror and looked at her reflection. There he saw her looking as beautiful as she really was and he saw the tears that were in her eyes.

"How can I help you?" he asked.

"It is dangerous," she said.

"I will dare any danger," he replied.

"There is a crystal ball," she said, "and only he who manages to survive all the dangers that surround it may obtain it. When the enchanter sees it, his power will be destroyed and the spell that binds me will be undone."

"I will find it. I will obtain it," the young man said confidently.

"Many men have died in the attempt."

"No man would have tried harder than I," he said passionately. "Tell me what I must do that I may start at once."

"At the foot of this mountain," the princess told him, "you will find a wild bull by a spring of water. You must fight it, and if you kill it a bird of fire will fly up from its body. The bird carries a red-hot egg in its body, and the yolk of that egg is the crystal ball. The bird will not want to lose the egg and will do everything in its power to keep it. If you manage to force it to drop it, however, you must be very careful, because if it falls on the earth it will start a blaze that will melt both the egg and the yolk and you will be left with nothing, and I will have lost my last chance to become myself again."

"I will be careful," the young man promised.

At the foot of the mountain he found the wild bull fearsomely pawing up the turf beside a spring of water, snorting and bellowing. He drew his sword and went in to the attack. With feint and spring and plunge he tried time and again to best the animal, and many a time he felt its hot breath on him and feared he was about to meet his death. But at last it was his thrust that won home and the beast fell to the ground. As it gave its last gasp a bird flew out of its mouth, as bright and hot as the sun, long plumes of flame trailing behind it.

The young man leapt up and tried to catch it, but could not.

Suddenly an eagle swooped down from the high blue sky and pursued it, snapping at it with its beak and reaching for it with its talons. At last the fire-bird was forced to drop its egg.

It fell on a fisherman's hut beside the sea. The hut immediately caught fire, but before the egg and yolk could melt a whale heaved its great bulk up close to the shore and caused a huge wave to break over the burning hut, extinguishing the flames.

The young man came running up and searched through the hot ashes. There he found the egg cracked and, within it, unharmed, the crystal ball.

He took it at once and confronted the enchanter.

The enchanter looking into the crystal found that he no longer had the powers he once had. Sighing, he told the young man that *he* was now to be the king in the Castle of the Golden Sun and the princess was free. The brother who had been an eagle and the brother who had been a whale were also free.

Rejoicing, the young man hurried to the princess and found her as he had seen her in the mirror.

There and then they exchanged rings.

Comment

A first glance this story seems to be concerned almost exclusively with the horrors of the night, the fear that the sun won" t rise in the morning, and the effort man has to make to ensure that it does. It harks right back to the ancient days of sun-worship.

The hero has to release the sun from the dark enchantments of the night. The beautiful sun looks old and dark and ugly, its true beauty only seen by looking into the mirror (the moon) which reflects its light. Twenty-three attempts have been made to rescue her, and if the twenty-fourth fails "she" will never rise again. We are speaking here of twenty-four hours, of course. The chambers the young man searches to find the princess are reminiscent of the twelve dark chambers of the night the sun-god Ra travels through in ancient Egyptian mythology, each one illuminated as Ra enters, but left dormant and dark when he leaves. The young man is following the sun through the dark chambers of the night, each one empty until the last.

The two giants? Could they be Night and Day fighting over who shall win? The fire-bird rises, trailing feathers of gold and flame like the sunrise, having been released from the powerful grip of the earth-bull. The whale that causes the wave to put out the unwanted fire reminds us of the moon pulling the waters of the ocean to make the tides. The eagle reminds us of Ra-Harakhti, Horus, the sun-god of Egypt.

That the sun is represented by a woman is interesting and suggests that the legend has its roots very far back in prehistory. In ancient matriarchal times the sun was always a woman. It is only in patriarchal times that the sun is exclusively male and the moon female.

The crystal ball itself? Is there some suggestion that the proper balance of night and day is dependent on finding the crystal ball which – certainly visually – reminds us of the moon? Without it, the sun cannot fulfil its role. We arc talking about interdependence here – the beautiful harmony of things working together.

Having noted all this, we find there are many more implications to the story that are worth exploring.

Here we have a harsh mother-figure who drives her sons away, apparently with great cruelty, forcing them to take on the role of an eagle, a whale, and a wolf or bear (though this fate the youngest son manages to escape, having learned from the experience of his brothers). She reminds me of Ceridwen and Arianrhod in the Welsh legends, both of whom drove their sons from them to battle against difficulties and suffer hardships, for them to emerge at last as fully realized men, wise and good rulers of the kingdom of themselves.

Ceridwen mixes up a concoction in a cauldron that will give great knowledge and wisdom to whoever has but one drop of it, Three drops spatter on to the thumb of the young boy who is stirring it. He sucks them off and instantly is the possessor of marvellous secrets. Furious that her gift has gone too soon and to the wrong person, she pursues him. He uses his new-found knowledge to become a hare. She pursues him as a hound. He becomes a fish and she pursues him as an otter. The fish leaps and becomes a bird. She is after him as an eagle. Finally he hides as one grain on a threshing floor of a million grains and thinks he is safe. But she, as a hen, pecks him up and swallows him. He is born nine months later from her body. She throws him into the sea in a leather bag, and when he is washed up on shore and found, it is as though he has been born three times. He grows up to he the mighty poet and seer Taliesin.

Arianrhod refuses to give her son a name and has to be tricked into it by her magician brother who has adopted the boy. Without a name given by the one who brought him into the world, without being acknowledged by her (accepted by her as a "chela" or novice), he cannot start on the path to the Higher Self and true wisdom. She refuses a second time to acknowledge him when he is about to enter manhood, and refuses to give him arms. Again she is tricked into it and in her rage she puts a curse on him – he is never to have a wife of the race that inhabits the earth. She condemns him to lifelong chastity. Her brother fashions a woman out of flowers for his bride. They marry, but it is not long before she plots his death with another man. He is "killed" in an elaborate, sacrificial way, but instead of dying is transformed into an eagle and flies away. Gwydion, his adopted father, searches the world for him and finds him at last only by following a sow which every day goes to the same place to feed off the rotting flesh that drops from a wounded eagle perching high in an oak tree. It is worth noting that the sow in Celtic legend is often the symbol of the Earth Mother, the Goddess – so it is likely that the sow here is a representation of Arianrhod, the goddess, who has harried her son enough and now allows him to return to his own form and his own lands – where he becomes "a good and wise ruler".

Ceridwen, Arianrhod, and the sorceress in the story of the crystal hall show a kind of divine, creative rage that many of the great fearsome goddesses of other cultures show: for example, Kali of India, Sekhmet of Egypt. Jehovah in Eden is playing the same role.

In Grimm's story of the crystal ball, the sorceress wants to keep her arcane knowledge from her sons, but they find a greater knowledge by being driven away from her. The one gains the knowledge of the "air" as eagle, symbolically the medium of the "supraconsciousness". It is he who releases the spirit-egg. The other gains the knowledge of "water", symbolically the depths of the subconscious. It is he who puts out the destructive fire caused by knowledge falling into "the wrong hands' (the fisherman's hut). How often have we felt "in our bones' – that is, in our sub-conscious – that we are not ready for something and so must stand back from it awhile? It is as though the subconscious provides us with a safety catch and warns us by intuition when the time is not right for a certain action.

The whale-brother uses water to put out the fire that is burning too fiercely for the good of the spirit-egg. The earth-brother, the one still in human form and representing the "middle" or ordinary consciousness, is thus enabled to search for it and find it when it is cool enough to touch, that is, when it is in a form that will be safe for him.

So we see it is uncertain whether the sorceress-mother is really as unloving, suspicious, and jealous as she appears, or whether she is a goddess setting severe initiation tests for her sons for their own good. The shape-changing into non-human form might be a way of teaching them things they would not be able to learn otherwise.

As always in myths, legends, and fairy stories, certain potent themes recur both within the fabric of the story itself and throughout the whole field or territory of the myth-maker.

We have seen that the mother who puts her sons through initiation is a common theme throughout the field. So is the princess in the tower to be rescued by an intrepid young man. Almost always the princess in the tower is the symbol of the Higher Self – that part of the young man's own being which is in a higher state of enlightenment than his "ordinary" self. The achievement of a state of marriage or union with her will lead him to the Higher Realms nearer to the ultimate source of life and light – to the Deity itself – the destination of all our struggling and our journeying. But only when the spiritual energy of the bird is released from the powerful earth-energy holding it down and represented by the bull, can the young man begin to contemplate achieving union with the princess.

It is important that the young man must have a change of consciousness before he can see the object of his aspiration as beautiful. When he first starts striving towards the new life he is still a victim of his ordinary consciousness and sees her as ugly; that is, we don't always see how desirable it is to reach towards the Light. She has to show him how to distinguish between reality and illusion. But he still fails without a tool of some kind (the mirror). Only at the end when he has won through everything does he see her as she really is without the help of the mirror.

But to return to the journey – before the final outcome is achieved. We notice that when the young man listened to others he couldn't find the castle and began to despair. The deep, dark forest in which he is lost corresponds to the "dark night of the soul" in mystical terms – the point furthest from hope where so often, having given up all expectation and preconceived ideas of what we are looking for, we suddenly find, unexpectedly (but not by accident), the way out. Who would have thought a "hat" would bring him to the castle? Any thing, at any time, can give us the spark of inspiration that sets us off in the right direction. We must despise nothing, but be open to wisdom wherever it might appear, in whatever guise. The "hat", of course, is something worn on the head, so implies some connection with the thinking process. The two giants fighting? Could it be two major religions tearing each other apart, trying to get at the truth, but losing it to a quiet little person who has the wit to see how to use it?

Every detail in this story is significant. The castle is at the top of a mountain. We have to aspire to union with our Higher Selves. The bull is at the bottom of the mountain. He represents the sexual desires the young man has to overcome if the bird of the spirit is to emerge. But note that he is waiting for the challenge of the young man beside a spring – a spring that comes out of the depths of the earth and brings life to a parched land. The bull has to be overcome or sacrificed beside a spring so that his blood will fertilize the land. The young man has sacrificed part of himself in order to be born again. The placenta (the bull) is left behind, the bird, the new birth, emerges and flies off carrying with it the cosmic egg that contains the crystal ball – the precious thing without which all his efforts would have been in vain. To be born again is not enough. The effort that went into it has to be sustained. The bird flies off carrying the egg of the young man's rebirth, He cannot have it if it falls back on to the earth. He has to reach up to it and catch it in flight. With the crystal ball inside it he has to confront the enchanter, and the distinction between illusion and reality will be made clear.

The sorceress had started a train of events that had led to transformation. With the defeat of the enchanter, the illusionist, the process is complete.

The young man has come this far by his own efforts. By his own wits he has found the Golden Castle and the princess, and by his courage and strength he has fought and overcome the bull. But now he needs help.

Another recurring theme in the mythic field is the theme of three – three gods, three brothers, three sisters. More often than not they represent three aspects of the one person.

Because this is a legend and not a "straight" story, each image in it can be interpreted in several different ways, the multi-layered meanings giving us endlessly nourishing food for thought.

The eagle, the far-seeing bird, pursues the fire-bird and makes it drop the egg. But the eagle does not only represent the supraconsciousness; it might also represent in this instance an aspect of the "middle" consciousness, the harsh, aggressive side of ourselves, the shrewd and alert side: the intellect. The gentle whale, living in the depths of the ocean of the subconscious, represents the intuitive, mystical side. It puts out the raging fire of ambition and allows us finally to reach the egg. Remember the young man had been boastful and overconfident: "I *will* find it!" he said. He needs the drive of the eagle, but also the caution of the whale.

At last the young man holds the crystal ball in his hand. What is the significance of this crystal ball? If it were possible to spell it out it would have been spelled out in the story. We can only hint or suggest what it might mean. It might mean, as in many other similar tales, that the enchanter has hidden his soul in the crystal ball to keep it safe from harm if he himself is attacked. Now, seeing that it is vulnerable, the enchanter loses his confidence and therefore his power. Or it might mean that the young man, by holding up the crystal ball to the enchanter, forces him to look into the depths of himself. Like the mirror, it does not lie, it shows what is there. He tried to avoid looking into himself by making the crystal so inaccessible – but he had reckoned without the persistent urge of the human being to seek purpose and find truth.

There are three young men, three brothers and a princess, released from danger and enchantment by the finding of this crystal ball. Does it represent the germ or quick of the cosmic egg – the growing point of the spirit from which all things spring?

According to Manly P. Hall in his marvellous book of eso-teric lore, *Secret Teachings of All Ages*, the crystal ball in general is a threefold symbol. It is at once "the crystalline Universal Egg in whose transparent depths creation exists", "the proper figure of Deity previous to Its immersion in matter", and "it signifies the aetheric sphere of the world in whose translucent essences is impressed and preserved the perfect image of all terrestrial activity". No wonder the lord of darkness gives up when faced with this!

It is worth noting in this connection that several icons of the angel Gabriel and the Christ show a crystal ball. Peter Lamborn Wilson in his book *Angels* says that the crystal ball in Gabriel's hand "seems to represent both the world – the outer display of God's magnitude, and the womb – the secret innerness of God's mercy".

All dark veils fall away as the young man of Grimm's story holds up the crystal ball to the enchanter: the sunlight breaks through with a blaze of glory as the young sun-goddess takes on her full splendour.

The lovers "exchange rings' – the symbol of eternity.

It is interesting that there is a sorceress and an enchanter. Are they the same person – the two sides, male and female, the yin and yang, of the Deity – both forcing the human being to the limits of his endurance, driving him to find his true and Higher Self, the eternal spirit within him – the female persecuting the male, the male persecuting the female – the dark trying to over-whelm the Light, the light trying to free itself from the dark – the tension between opposites that drives the world on its way?

Sources

Jacob and Wilhelm Grimm, *Selected Tales*, translated by David Luke (Penguin Classics, 1982), story no. 53. (Story no. 197, "Die Kristallkugel" in original 1850 Grimm edition.)

Manly P. Hall, *Secret Teachings of All Ages*: And *Encyclopedic Outline of Masonic, Hermetic, Qabhalistic and Rosicrucian Symbolical Philosophy*, Section C (1901; The Philosophical Research Society, Inc., Los Angeles, 1977).

Peter Lamborn Wilson, *Angels* (Thames & Hudson, 1980) facing p. 28.

The Mabinogion, translated by Lady Charlotte Guest (J M Dent & Co., 1906). For the story of Arianrhod see "Math the Son of Mathonwy", and for the story of Ceridwen see "Taliesin".

Chapter 4

The Ring of Invisibility

(Western Europe: Arthurian)

One day at Arthur's court, one of the knights, Kynan, told the story of how he had been bested by a fearsome knight dressed in black armour and guarding a spring. Kynan's tale of the magical events and the twenty-four beautiful women that led up to the encounter, interested the knight Owein, and he boasted that if he had challenged the Black Knight the outcome would have been different. Sir Kei's sharp reply that he was a man more for his speeches than for his deeds, spurred him on to seek out the Black Knight and prove Kei wrong.

Following Kynan's instructions, Owein set off for "the far reaches and the desolate mountains of the world".

He found the beautiful and fertile valley Kynan had told him about and the fortress with the hospitable lord and twenty-four fair maidens, who waited upon him and presented him with a delicious meal.

He enquired about the spring and was given instructions as to how to find it.

He rode as Kynan had done into the forest, and there in a clearing, seated on a mound, he found the Keeper of the Forest, a giant swarthy man with one eye and one leg, holding a huge iron spear. Around him hundreds of different animals grazed peacefully with one another.

From him Owein took direction to the spring as Kynan had done before him.

"Take the path from this clearing and climb the hill you will see. From the summit you will look over a valley and at the centre of it there is a great tree. Beneath the tree is a spring of fresh water and beside it is a stone slab to which a silver bowl is chained. Fill the bowl with water and throw the water on the stone."

All these instructions Owein followed, and when he found the huge and spreading oak in the valley he found the spring beneath it and, beside it, the slab of stone with the silver cup.

He filled the cup with water and splashed it on the stone.

Instantly there was a deafening clap of thunder, followed by a deluge of rain and hail. The hailstones were as big as a man's fist and drove into his flesh with extraordinary force. He only survived by covering himself and his horse's head with his shield, and pulling his vizor down.

When the storm abated and he lifted his shield and vizor he saw that the great tree had been stripped of all its leaves, but the sky was a brilliant blue. Birds alighted in the tree and sang more sweetly than he had ever heard birds sing before.

Suddenly the knight Kynan had encountered appeared, accoutred all in black, on a fierce black charger. They fought long and hard, and at length Owein struck him such a blow that the Black Knight knew that he was mortally wounded. He turned his horse and withdrew from the battle.

Owein followed him until at length they came to a glittering city and a strong fortress. The portcullis was raised at once for the Black Knight, but when Owein tried to follow him it was lowered suddenly. His horse was cut in two and he himself was caught between the two gates, unharmed, but a prisoner.

The people of the fortress were so preoccupied with the Black Knight and his wounds, that Owein was left where he was, knowing that when he was found it would be the worse for him.

At last he saw someone walking down the street outside the fortress. It was a young woman with golden curls and a gold headband, dressed in yellow satin, with shoes of many-coloured leather.

She asked for the gate to be opened and he explained his predicament. It seemed she remembered him from Arthur's court and knew that he was a man of honour. She told him that her name was Luned and she offered him her help. She presented him with a gold ring set with a large crystal.

"Take this ring and put it on your finger," she said. "Turn the crystal so that it is concealed in your hand. As long as you conceal it, it will conceal you."

He accepted it with gratitude and did as she said.

"When they come to take you to put you to death," she continued, "they will think that you have already escaped and open the gates. I will be there. Come to me at once and put your hand on my shoulder. I'll not be able to see you, but will feel your hand. I'll lead you to safety."

All happened as Luned had predicted, and she led Owein away to a chamber in the city where she bathed his head with water from a silver bowl and served him a delicious meal. She then suggested he rest on a bed of fine linen and soft furs.

As he dozed off he heard a cry from the fortress and asked Luned what it was. "They are anointing the knight who owns the fortress," she replied.

Owein slept, but at midnight woke to hear another fearful cry.

"The knight of the fortress has died," Luned told Owein and hushed him to sleep again.

Just before dawn he woke to a tumult in the streets.

Again Luned enlightened him. They were taking the dead knight to church to bury him. Owein went to the window and gazed down at the procession. Behind the bier was a woman with golden hair, a golden headband, and a dress of yellow satin with blood upon it. Her shoes were of many-coloured leather. Her face was pale and she wrung her hands pitifully, weeping all the while.

Owein asked Luned who she was and the young woman replied: "She is the Lady of the Spring, my mistress, the wife of the knight you killed yesterday."

"God knows," Owein said. "I love her."

Then Luned took out a bowl of water and an ivory razor and shaved the young knight. Later she fed him again, and again told him to sleep.

"I will go courting on your behalf," she said, and left him in the chamber alone.

Luned went to the fortress and spoke with her mistress, persuading her that it would be foolish to spend the time fruitlessly mourning her lord; she should find another husband who was capable of defending her and her spring. The lady eventually agreed, and Luned said she would go to Arthur's court to find a suitable knight.

When she returned so soon with Owein clad all in yellow and gold apart from his shoes of many-coloured leather, the lady became suspicious and suggested that he was the man who had killed her husband. But still Luned managed to persuade her that he would be the right man to marry. "For," she said, "so much the better for you, my lady. If this man were not superior to your husband, he would not have overcome him."

The lady, still hesitating, asked her subjects what she should do, and they agreed a strong man was needed to guard the spring, for the realm depended on it.

She took Owein to her bed, and for three years he guarded the spring for her as the Black Knight had done before him.

After three years Arthur and Kei and several of the other knights came in search of Owein. They followed the route Kynan had told them about and came at last to the tree and the spring.

There Kei was challenged by a knight in black armour and thrown to the ground.

That night Arthur and his companions camped nearby and in the morning Kei challenged the Black Knight again. Again he was bested. Then every one of Arthur's company went against the guardian of the spring and was thrown down, until only two were left undefeated, Gawain and Arthur himself.

Gawain asked to go first and Arthur agreed.

The two knights fought for three days but neither could overthrow the other.

At the end of the third day a blow to the head of Gawain displaced his helmet and Owein recognized his cousin for the first time. Then he revealed who he was and the two bowed to each other, each offering the other his weapon in token of his surrender to the better knight. But Arthur took the swords of both knights in his own hands so that neither would have to surrender to the other, and embraced them both.

Delighted to see his old companions again, Owein invited them all back to his fortress, where he and his wife entertained them for three years. At the end of that time Arthur persuaded her to let him take Owein back to his own court for a visit of three months. The lady was reluctant to let him go – but she agreed at last on the understanding that it would he for no more than three months.

Owein, however, stayed on at Arthur's court for three years, forgetting all about his wife and the spring he was supposed to guard.

One day a beautiful young woman rode into the court, dressed all in yellow and gold, even her horse's saddle of gold. She rode right into the hall and up to Owein. She reached down and pulled the ring from his finger, calling him a "treacherous deceiver". He had scarcely realized what was happening before she turned her horse and was gone.

Then Owein was stricken with shame, for he remembered his vows and how he had betrayed them.

He left Arthur's court and wandered into the wilderness in the far reaches and the desolate mountains of the world. His clothes fell off and he did not care. His hair grew long and he kept company with wild animals.

Slowly he grew too weak to keep up with them, and wandered out of the mountains on to a fertile plain.

There he was seen sleeping on the ground, filthy and covered in sores, by a widowed countess out walking with her handmaidens. Shocked to see a human being reduced to such a wild state, the countess arranged for ointment and clothes and a horse to be left near the creature. One of the handmaidens stayed to watch what happened and helped him back to the castle. There he was carefully tended for three months. At the end of that time he was back to his former shade and shape.

The castle was attacked by an enemy, and Owein asked the handmaiden who had been caring for him to provide him with armour and a horse as he wanted to help defend her mistress.

He fought with his former valour and defeated the invader easily.

The widow wanted to reward him and keep him with her, but he refused. Still nursing the regret and shame for his desertion of the Lady of the Spring, he wandered off again into the wilderness.

There one day he came upon a cliff, in the cleft of which was a gigantic serpent, and beside the serpent a lion. Whenever the lion attempted to leave, the serpent lunged at it and cut off its retreat.

Owein dismounted at once and attacked the serpent with his sword, destroyed it, and rode on.

Later he realized the lion was following him like a pet greyhound, and from that time on it stayed with him day and night, hunting for him and bringing him meat.

One night he heard someone moaning and discovered a young girl held in a stone prison. It was Luned, whose fortunes had suffered a severe setback when her protégé proved to be so false. She had been flung into this cage by two men when she had defended Owein against their jeering, and they had said they would leave her there for so many days, and if Owein himself did not come to rescue her by the last day specified they would kill her.

Luned then directed Owein to a nearby castle, where he was made welcome, but finding everyone doleful and sad he enquired what the matter was. It seemed there was an evil brute in the mountains who had stolen the earl's two sons and would kill them that very day if he did not send his daughter to him.

Owein at once armed himself and fought the brute – but it was only with the help of the lion that he prevailed.

Then Owein refused the grateful lord's invitation to stay and be rewarded and hurried back to Luned. He was just in time to rescue her from being burnt to death by the two men who had imprisoned her. Again, it was only with the help of the lion that he succeeded.

Luned led him back to the Lady of the Spring.

He took her to Arthur's court, where she was his only wife as long as she lived.

Comment

The ring of invisibility seems to have a very small part to play in this story, but actually it is crucial. Note that Owein is given it at the lowest point of his life. He is a prisoner awaiting execution. Note also that it is taken away when he has failed to live up to his responsibilities and fulfil his commitments. Luned rides her horse into the court of King Arthur and takes it back, telling him in no uncertain terms why she is doing so. In receiving and in losing it his life changes radically.

Up to the point of receiving the ring the young knight has been an adventurer on the purely physical plane. He is good at fighting, and sets off to fight the Black Knight simply because he has been insulted and told that he couldn't and wouldn't do it. He has no idea who the Black Knight is, nor does he care.

He is set on his course by the Keeper of the Forest – and again he does not quite grasp the significance of the encounter.

He mortally wounds his opponent and follows him – blindly.

At the portcullis, the double gate, he is brought up short. His horse, representing all that he had relied on before, is killed, and he is alone, awaiting death.

Luned appears. Note that her description matches that of her mistress. Both women have golden curls, and are dressed identically in yellow and gold. In Christian terms I see the mistress as the Deity, Luned as the Christ, the ring as the Holy Spirit. With the ring Owein disappears from the material world and enters the spiritual one – led by Christ first to safety and then to union with the Deity.

In pagan terms I see the mistress as the sun-goddess, Luned as her reflection, the moon, and the ring as the symbol of cyclical Nature. It will save him, if he saves it. John Rhys in his book *The Arthurian Legend* (p. 89) says: "The ring... refers to the disk of the sun with its light overpowering the strength of human vision and concealing the body of that luminary from the unaided eye of man." Presumably because Owein has been chosen to work with the sun for the good of Nature he now takes on the qualities of the sun-deity.

I am reminded of the warning the Israelites were given in the Sinai desert: they should not look on the face of the Lord or they would be blinded. The old idea of the Deity as the sun dies hard.

The wild man, the Keeper of the Forest, could, in Christian terms, be John the Baptist – pointing the way for the seeker to go to find the Saviour. John lived in the wilderness close to Nature. The peaceful feeding of the animals in his vicinity presages the holy time when "the lion will lie down with the lamb". The more ancient, pagan, underpinning of the story refers to Cernunnos, or maybe even an older nature god.

Black is not always the colour of evil or death. It is also the colour of "not knowing", not understanding, "being in the dark". In ancient Egypt it was actually the colour of life because it was the rich black silt from the yearly inundation of the Nile that brought life to the grainfields of the country. The name of Egypt in ancient times was Khemet – "the Black Land".

Here, in the Celtic story, the Master of the Forest is swarthy, black, because he is the mysterious unknown force behind Nature. Why is he one-eyed and one-legged? Perhaps "one" is used here in the sense of wholeness, singleness. There is no duality in his being. The eye is in the centre of this forehead where normally we consider the "third eye", the eye of clairvoyance, to be. He sees as a unified force, and he moves as a unified force. He is frightening in a sense – yet he does not harm the knight who is seeking his encounter with the Otherworld. The animals love and respect him and feel safe under his care.

He sits on a mound. The ancient burial mounds were always believed to be places of powerful magic where it was possible to encounter the gods or beings of the other realms.

Owein reaches the spring. The most common name of the story as a whole is "The Lady (or Countess) of the Fountain". But whether spring, well, or fountain, the implications are the same. We are dealing with the "life's blood" of the earth, the spring of fresh water that keeps the land and its inhabitants alive, and at the same time represents the welling up of the spirit from beneath the encrustation of material reality. It is the source of spiritual renewal to which Owein must go, albeit at first unknowingly and from the wrong motives, before he can become a fully realized being in union with his Deity. The water wells up beneath a tree – a particularly magnificent tree standing out above all other trees – the Tree of Life.

The water, the life-giving substance, cannot be obtained without a struggle. The Black Knight must be challenged, and only he who overcomes him can drink. As always, deep esoteric teaching is guarded from those who have nothing more than idle curiosity – from the foolish and weak and evil, from those who are not ready for it. We have to win it and prove that we are capable of using it responsibly.

Are the Black Knight and the wild man, the Keeper of the Forest, connected? They are both "black", as Luned and her mistress are both golden-yellow. The one is the black rich earth out of which Nature burgeons, the other the night, the storm, the rain-god. One is the nurturing side of the Deity, the other the dark and challenging side.

In pagan terms, the three forces, the golden sun, the rainstorm, the earth, are part of the same life-force. Owein has blundered into the cosmic drama that keeps all life in balance. If he upsets it he must restore it. If he kills the Black Knight, he must take his place. The spring must be protected at all costs. When he shirks his duty and goes back to Arthur's court, forgetting his commitment and responsibility, he is punished by having the ring, the key that opens the door to the Otherworld and the invisible realms where glorious spiritual adventures may occur, ignominiously removed. With its removal he realizes what he has lost and enters a period of deep despair and shame – the "dark night of the soul" – out of which he can only come by regaining all the ground he had lost – and more. The incident with the serpent and the lion is crucial. He has to rescue his inner and higher power and strength (the lion) from his lower nature (the serpent), for it is only with it that he can undo the harm he has done to Luned (the Christ) and reunite with the Deity.

The theme of the ring or stone of invisibility is a common one in legends and myths throughout the world.

In another Celtic legend from the *Mabinogion* Peredur is given a stone by a shining lady on a green mound which renders him invisible so that he can fight and defeat a dangerous monster.

In Southern Africa there is a folk belief in a little creature called a Tokoloshe, a dangerous dwarf – often the familiar of witches and sorcerers. For a long while this creature, though inimical to adults, was friendly towards children. One day a child stole its pebble of invisibility. Instantly invisible, the child spent all day teasing the Tokoloshe until at last the dwarf burst into tears, knowing that without the pebble he would not be able to function. The child, no doubt tired of the game, felt pity and returned the little stone to the Tokoloshe. It is said that from that time on the Tokoloshe of Southern Africa have kept themselves invisible and have been as wary of children as they are of adults.

In the *Republic* (359) Plato told the story of Gyges, a Lydian shepherd of the seventh century BC, who stumbled into a chasm which opened up suddenly after an earthquake. There he found a huge bronze horse. He opened a panel in its side and saw the body of a man. He took the ring from the finger of the corpse and fled.

Later he was with some companions and idly turned the ring round on his finger so that the jewel was on the palm side of his hand. He noticed to his surprise that his companions appeared no longer to be able to see him. He experimented and discovered the secret of the ring. He arranged to be one of the delegation of shepherds that visited the palace and succeeded in seducing the queen. With the ring's help and hers, he murdered the king, married the queen and took the throne.

Plato uses the story to illustrate a point he wants to make. What if there were two such rings, he suggests – one worn by a just man and one by an unjust man? Would the just man, knowing that he could not be found out, do just as many "unjust" things as the unjust man? How often do we not wish that we could observe without being observed, and enjoy all the advantages of being involved in action without any of the disadvantages? Is a sense of morality intrinsic to human nature, or is it something imposed by society and easily shed?

It is interesting in the story of Owein and Luned that Owein apparently does not use the ring apart from that one time, and that to escape death. Is this an oversight on the part of the storyteller, or an indication that a part of the story has been lost over the centuries? Or is Owein such a just man (in Plato's sense) that it does not enter his head to take advantage of the ring for nefarious purposes? Perhaps it is because, in this case, the ring is not a ring in the Gygean or Tokoloshe sense, capable of conferring physical invisibility only, but a key to the invisible realms of the spirit.

The whole story, as any good legend will, works on many different levels simultaneously. The mention of twenty-four maidens (hours), the frequent contrasting of black characters and gold characters, suggests that the story originated in very ancient times when the rising of the sun each day was not taken for granted, but had to be prayed for, sacrificed for, brought about by human effort. In ancient Egypt the walls of tombs were richly decorated with representations of the sun's nightly journey through the dark underworld and the dangers it faced there in its battle with Apep, the monstrous serpent that represented extinction, non-existence. Our own survival is intimately bound up with the sun's – physically if we take it only as a physical object, but spiritually too if we take it as the cipher for the Deity otherwise beyond our imagining.

It is Owein's reunion with the sun-goddess that is the culmination of all his struggles. In the story we get a more vivid picture of Luned and her unselfish and unpossessive love for Owein, than we do of the Lady of the Spring. I have to confess on several occasions I wished Owein would take Luned to wife instead of her mistress. But I was missing the point of the difference between the guide and the goal. We have a closer working relationship with our guide, our teacher, than we do with the remote luminary towards which we are aspiring.

Sources

The Mabinogion, translated by Jeffrey Gantz: "The Countess of the Fountain" (Penguin Books, 1976).

The Mabinogion, translated by Lady Charlotte Guest: "The Lady of the Fountain" (J. M. Dent & Co., 1906).

Bulfinch's Mythology. The Age of Chivalry; Part II: "The Lady of the Fountain" (The Modern Library, New York).

John Rhys, *The Arthurian Legend* (The Clarendon Press, Oxford, 1891).

Chapter 5

The Two Swords of Galahad

(Western Europe: Arthurian)

One: The Sword in the Stone

On a day four hundred and fifty years after the birth of Christ, the knights were gathered at Camelot for a feast, when a page reported seeing a great wonder, a boulder floating down the river. Ever eager for marvels the company followed him at once, and found a great chunk of red marble lying on the river bank, and within it, held fast, was a magnificent sword, "with a pommel carved from a precious stone cunningly inlaid with letters of gold". The inscription read: "None shall take me from this stone except the best knight in the world."

The knights at once urged Lancelot to try to draw the sword out, saying that he was without doubt the best knight in the world. But he refused, saying that he had a premonition that it would be dangerous for the wrong person to attempt the task. He said that he had the feeling that this day would be a special day – the beginning of a High Adventure greater than any ever undertaken by the knights of Arthur's Round Table before.

The king ordered Sir Gawain and Sir Perceval to attempt to draw the sword out, but when this failed, they gave up and returned to the castle, leaving the sword and the stone on the river bank.

While they were at meat, suddenly the doors and windows of the castle slammed shut, though there was no wind. Before the chair of Arthur stood an old, old man leading a youth by the hand. He was clad in red armour but carried neither sword nor shield.

"I bring you one for whom you have waited," the old man said. "One who stems from the House of David and the line of Joseph of Arimathea."

The court greeted the youth warmly, impressed by his lineage and his fair countenance that bore a striking resemblance to that of Lancelot. They invited him to join the feast, and without more ado he sat in the seat that had stood empty since the Round Table had first been assembled, the seat that had been called "Perilous", for until this time whoever had sat upon it had met with some ill fate. Mysteriously letters had appeared on it, and the letters spelled his name, Galahad, the son of Lancelot by the daughter of the Fisher King, until this time unknown to Lancelot. The court knew by this sign that the numbers of the knights who would embark on the greatest Adventure they had ever known was now complete.

It was no surprise to them that it was Galahad who drew the sword from the stone on the river bank. They knew it was his sword.

On the day of Pentecost the knights were gathered to celebrate the memory of the time the Holy Ghost descended on the disciples and illuminated their minds with tongues of fire.

Suddenly the hall was filled with a blaze of light and all fell silent, looking from one to another, awed and uneasy. And then – and then the Holy Grail appeared, "covered with a cloth of white samite; and yet no mortal hand was seen to bear it. It entered through the great door, and at once the palace was filled with fragrance as though all the spices of the earth had been spilled abroad. It circled the hall along the great tables and each place was furnished in its wake with the food its occupants desired. When all were served, the Holy Grail vanished, they knew not how nor whither" (*The Quest of the Holy Grail*, p. 44).

This was the beginning of the Great Quest and the breaking up of the company of the Round Table, for many a knight who was present at the time vowed to leave Camelot and devote the rest of his life to seeking the Grail. "For this is no search for earthly things but a seeking out of the mysteries and hidden sweets of Our Lord, and the divine secrets which the most high Master will disclose to that blessed knight whom He has chosen for His servant from among the ranks of chivalry: he to whom He will show the marvels of the Holy Grail, and reveal that which the heart of man could not conceive nor tongue relate" (*The Quest of the Holy Grail*, p. 47).

Comment

The stories of the search for the Holy Grail are complex and numerous. Here we are concerned only with the story of the sword with the crystal pommel – in fact, with the two swords of Galahad, each received in mysterious circumstances, and each with a crystal pommel.

That Galahad is of the line of Joseph of Arimathea, who was the uncle of Jesus Christ and the man who took Him down from the Cross and buried him in his own family tomb, makes him of particular interest. The implication is that Galahad is related by ancestry to the Lord Christ, presumably through his grandfather, the Fisher King.

The Grail legends are very rich in difficult symbolic concepts, partly because they are trying to express the inexpressible, and partly because they had been handed down orally from very ancient pagan Celtic times before they were retold and written down by Christians, in France, in Germany, in Britain. No one knows exactly who the author of *The Quest of the Holy Grail* is. It may have been a compilation of many authors writing at many different times. But one thing is certain: it may be difficult to follow a logical path through it, but it lifts the spirit and excites the imagination wonderfully.

The wounding of the Fisher King brought about the creation of a Waste Land in a formerly green and fertile country. To heal him, and consequently heal the land, is a sacred task the knights attempt. That the king is referred to as the "Fisher" King links him to Christ, who was the fisher of men. That the land is laid waste by his wounding indicates, on a spiritual level, that our "wounding" of Christ by our evil deeds does not only harm him, but everything else in our lives as well. But the legend is more ancient than the New Testament. In pagan times it was believed that anything wrong with the king would reflect itself in the land.

The Grail itself, which feeds each and every knight with the food of his choice, indicates that the holy secret of the Word is understood by each and every person according to his or her own stage of development, and gives the nourishment he or she particularly needs. The chalice from which the holy wine is drunk – and the Grail is often referred to as a chalice (though also sometimes as a luminous precious stone) – harks back to the cauldron of plenty of the ancient Celts: the cauldron of the Earth Mother that feeds the teeming millions; the cauldron of Ceridwen in which she brews the wisdom of the sages; the cauldron of Bran, the Blessed, that restores dead warriors to life.

Galahad is a Christ-figure, but also a Solar Hero; he performs magical acts and miracles of healing, linking these medieval legends not only to the Christ and the great and ancient days of David and Solomon, but to the very oldest religion, the Mysteries of the Earth.

"Galahad... you are the lily of purity, you are the true rose, the flower of strength and healing with the tint of fire; for the fire of the Holy Ghost burns in you so brightly that my flesh which was withered and dead is now made young and strong again." Thus said the wounded King Mordrain to the knight Galahad (*The Quest of the Holy Grail* p. 269).

Before we read about the second sword of Galahad there are certain things to bear in mind about the first. Note that the first is buried in stone and comes floating down a river. The stone is the earth, material reality. Galahad has to free his will, his power, his spirit from the prison of earthly concerns. That a stone that should sink in water floats, is an indication that we are dealing with the supernatural and not the natural. The second sword of Galahad is lying on a bed.

The Grail when first glimpsed is covered with a veil of white samite. Later, when it appears on the ship of Solomon, it is covered with red samite. I assume this is because the veil has been stained with the blood of the sacrificial tasks Galahad has performed between one sighting and the next.

Two: The Sword of David

Three knights from King Arthur's Round Table, Sir Galahad, Sir Perceval, and Sir Bors, are involved in an extraordinary experience connected with the sword of David.

Sir Galahad, the pure and noble son of Sir Lancelot, is led by a beautiful maiden through a forest to the sea shore. There he finds his two friends, Bors and Perceval, beside a ship. The maiden tells them that if they are seeking a High Adventure they must embark on this ship. Eagerly they climb aboard and are carried out into the ocean. They have no control over the ship, which seems to have a mind of its own. Eventually they come to a remote island and the ship comes to a halt. They see before them another ship, more splendid than the first. It is clear that they have been brought here for a purpose, and the young maiden urges them to read what is engraved in Chaldean on the side of the new ship: "Take care whoever sets foot on me that he is full of faith."

The companions hesitate, for the inscription ends with many a dire warning as to what will happen if one's faith should waver.

Galahad, knowing that his faith is strong, takes the first step, and the others follow.

On board they find no living soul, but a chamber with a magnificent bed draped in white silk. A golden crown is at its head, and three unusual posts shaped like spindles of white, green, and red wood at its foot. On the bed itself lies a sword half out of a snakeskin scabbard.

On closer inspection they find further inscriptions which warn that no one will be able to grip the pommel of this sword unless he is the Chosen One. Only one man in all time will be able to wield it without harm to himself, and he will be pure in heart and steadfast in faith beyond all other men.

"The sword was very curiously fashioned: for the pommel was formed of a stone combining all the colours found on earth; and, for another and greater singularity, each colour had its own specific virtue" (*The Quest of the Holy Grail*, p. 214). The hilt was double ribbed, the one rib fashioned from the bones of a Caledonian serpent which ensured that whoever held it could not feel heat, and the other from the bones of a fish that came from the river Euphrates and whose property it was to ensure that anyone who took hold of it would become totally single-minded in purpose and forget everything else except the one purpose for which the sword had been gripped.

Perceval and Bors both tried to grip the sword, but failed.

The young maiden told them horrific tales of how other men had tried to lift the sword and succeeded, but because they were not the Chosen One for whom the sword was waiting, they had met injury and death. At one time it had even been snapped in half at a critical moment in order that it would not be used by an unworthy knight, only to heal itself miraculously when he left it alone.

The young knights remarked that the belt on which the re-markable and magnificent sword was fitted was of common hemp and totally out of place on such a weapon. The maiden explained that part of the destiny of the sword would be fulfilled when that belt was replaced by another, more suitable one fashioned by a young virgin, the daughter of both a king and queen. She told them that at Pentecost she had foreseen that this was her destiny, and to show her acceptance of it she had shaved off her long golden locks and vowed to remain a virgin dedicated to holy works all her life. She opened the casket she had been carrying all this while and revealed a belt worthy of such a sword. It was woven of gold thread and her own golden hair. The whole length of it was studded with rare and precious gems.

Still hesitating to touch the sword, Galahad questioned her about the sword's history. It seems it had once belonged to King David. One day King David's son, King Solomon, "who was wise with all the knowledge that could be grasped by human understanding" and who "knew the powers of every precious stone, the virtues of all the herbs, and had a more perfect knowledge of the course of the firmament and of the stars than any saving God Himself", had a vision that the end of his line would bring to the world great and wonderful joy. This man, born of a woman of Solomon's line, would live about two thousand years after Solomon. So moved was the king by this vision that he grieved to think he would not be able to tell the man how he had foreseen his birth so many centuries before. Solomon's wife, who was as shrewd and cunning as her husband was wise, devised an elaborate scheme whereby the man would know his destiny and know that his ancestor had foreseen it all.

She advised Solomon to build a ship of hard and enduring wood, and in a chamber in the ship, to build a bed. His own golden crown was to be at the head of it, and at the base there were to be three wooden spindles carved from the Tree of Life. This tree had grown from the twig Eve had snatched off when she picked the fatal apple. It had taken root where she had placed it on the ground and grown beautiful beyond words over the centuries. At first its wood was pure white because it had been planted when Eve was still a virgin. When Adam and Eve made love under it for the first time and conceived their son Abel, the wood turned green. Later it was under this very tree that Cain murdered his brother Abel, and the wood of the tree turned blood-red.

On the bed would be laid King David's sword that had lain since his death in the Great Temple Solomon had built in Jerusalem. It would lie in the ship in readiness for the knight who would be the One Solomon saw in his vision – but before it was placed there, there was work to be done on it.

"'Take it and strip it of its hilt and pommel, so that we are left with the naked steel," she said. "And you who know the powers of stones, and the virtues of herbs, and the nature of all other things on earth, you must fashion a pommel of precious stones so cunningly joined that after your time no human eye shall be able to discern the seams, but all who look on it shall think it is entire. Next you must make a hilt of such extraordinary virtue that it shall have no equal in the world. And after, do you make a sheath worthy in all respects of such a sword. When you have done all this I shall provide a belt after my own liking'" (*The Quest of the Holy Grail*, p. 232).

Solomon fashioned the pommel and the hilt and the sheath, and the sword was ready for the belt. But when they came to lay it on the bed Solomon saw that his wife had made a belt of common hemp. She claimed she had nothing worthy of the belt, but a maiden would appear one day, when the time was ripe, who would.

She then ordered the spindles to be carved of the three different-coloured woods of the Tree of Life.

When the ship was finished it was clear that so many symbols had been worked into it that no one but the rightful one would ever be able to figure them out.

That night Solomon dreamed he saw angels visit the ship and sprinkle it with water from a silver chalice. Then they inscribed words on the sword and on the side of the ship. In the morning the words were where Solomon expected them to be and remained there for Galahad to read two thousand years later.

At last Galahad was ready. He placed his hand on the pommel and lifted the sword easily.

The maiden spoke the name of the sword: "Sword of the Strange Belt." And the name of the scabbard, she said, was "Memory of Blood".

She undid the sword that hung at Galahad's side and fastened on King David's sword, It was clear to all of them that he was the one for whom the sword had waited. And later it was clear that he, of all men the purest and most noble, would be the one to look into the cup of the Holy Grail and see the face of God.

Years later, after many spiritual trials and tests, the three companions were brought back to the ship where Galahad had received the "Sword of the Strange Belt", but this time they found there a silver table on which the Grail rested, covered by a veil of red samite. No sooner were they on board than a wind sprang up and the ship started to move. For how many weeks or months they were driven over the ocean they could not tell, but all the while Galahad lay sleeping on the bed King Solomon had prepared for him.

When the ship came to harbour at last and Galahad awoke, he found himself in the city of Sarras. There he healed cripples and performed many miracles. The king, uneasy about the strange knights, threw them into a dungeon. A year passed before he, on his deathbed, called for them and asked for their forgiveness.

Then was Galahad made king in his stead.

He made an "ark of gold and precious stones' to house the holy vessel on the silver table.

For a year the three prayed before the hidden Grail until at last Galahad was ready for the event towards which his whole life had been leading. A vision of Josephus, the son of Joseph of Arimathea, came to him and encouraged him to look directly into the Grail.

What he saw there no one knows but a trembling seized him and his face was radiant with ecstasy.

This was his last act on earth.

Comment

In the terms of the medieval legends connected with King Arthur's Round Table and the Quest for the Holy Grail a "High Adventure" meant an adventure of the spirit. Everything that happened in the story as it was told that seemed to be happening on the earthly plane (Malkut in kabbalistic terms) was not happening physically at all, but was part of a drama played out in the Higher Realms. Mountains were not mountains, forests were not forests, and ships were not ships. Maidens who waited under trees and then led a knight to his High Adventure were messengers from the Higher Realms – goddesses, angels, spirits...

There are two ships in this Adventure. The first is to take the three knights from the distractions of the mundane world and put them in a frame of mind conducive to making the most of what enlightenment will come their way.

There are three knights, as there are usually three brothers or three sisters in legends. I believe these refer to three levels of consciousness in the one individual. Only the one, the highest, will succeed in the Adventure.

The second ship, waiting for them beside an unknown island, far away from any land they know, is where the Adventure will occur. Galahad is the one for whom the Adventure will prove to be most rewarding, for he has been led this far by the mysterious maiden. The other two are ready and willing, but they had found the first ship almost by accident and were puzzling what to do when they were joined by Galahad and the maiden, who took the lead.

The second ship carries a dire warning that it would be dangerous to enter without faith. We find this kind of warning everywhere between the worlds and it always should be heeded. These high spiritual matters are dangerous to those who are not ready.

It is interesting to muse, in reading about the dilemma of Solomon, who wanted to communicate with his descendant two thousand years hence, that it is much the same dilemma faced by the space scientists in our own century when they were sending out a Voyager machine to travel through space and hopefully reach another inhabited planet countless light-years from us. Neither could rely on words. Both had to use visual symbols that could be understood in any time and any place by any kind of alien being.

Solomon's ship is a puzzle, the solving of which will be of vital importance to Galahad.

There are so many questions to ask, he must have wondered where to begin.

Why the ship? Why the bed? Why the crown? Why the three posts like spindles in the three very specific and different colours – yet from one tree. Why, above all, the sword on the bed? One does not usually leave one's sword lying about on a bed. Then once we get to the sword we have to ask more questions about it. Why the extraordinary pommel of different-coloured crystals fashioned so cunningly it looks as though it is made of one multicoloured crystal? Why the ribs of those particular bones? Why the snakeskin scabbard and the paltry belt of hemp? There is no end to the questions, and it is likely that only Galahad, for whom this whole elaborate and secret message was devised, could answer them all correctly. We can only ponder a while and see what we can find.

The ship? Some might say, since this is predominantly a Christian legend, that the ship represents the Church. If it does I would say it is the hidden, esoteric aspect of the Church that is represented, rather than the exoteric dogma and buildings. It is the sacred place, cut off from the world, in which one can journey to the Higher Realms.

The bed? A bed suggests sleep and rest – that quiet time in which one can enter other realities. It also suggests love-making, conception, fertility, life. These are not contradictory concepts as they might at first appear. A period of bodily rest from worldly activities often leads to the conception of ideas and visions. In fact P. M. Matarasso, in her illuminating notes to the translation of the text I have been quoting from, suggests that the bed might represent the altar of sacrifice, or – and this interpretation I join her in preferring – a place of ecstatic vision (p. 303).

The bed might also suggest the long blood-line from Galahad to Solomon. The crown is above the bed. This is a royal heir conceived in Solomon's bed.

The crown? The Chosen One is royal, the inheritor of Solomon's crown. As the wisdom of Solomon is stressed, it is likely that the crown also suggests that the Chosen One is the inheritor of Solomon's wisdom. Wisdom is usually associated with the crown of the head. The crown hangs at the head of the bed to emphasize this point.

The three posts so specifically made in the shape of spindles out of the three colours of wood? Three incidents have affected the colour of the Tree of Life. Note that it is not the wood from the original Tree of Life in Eden that is used, but wood from a cutting from it. All the incidents connected with it are "human-made" as it were. A bed needs four posts – the fourth incident will be the arrival of the Chosen One, White is for virginity and innocence. Galahad is virginal and innocent. Green is for fertility. Galahad embodies life and is reminiscent of Abel, the noble first-born son of Adam and Eve conceived under the tree. Red is for blood. Galahad is of the blood royal of the line of Solomon. He is also a Christian warrior who will use the sword to spill the blood of the unrighteous. Of all the characters in the Arthurian legends, Galahad is nearest to the concept of Christ, who gave himself in sacrifice like an ancient king.

Why spindles? The tree grew from the action of Eve, a woman. Spindles are associated with the work of women. Spinning and weaving are widely used traditional symbols associated with fate and destiny. In classical myth we have the three Fates spinning the thread of fate. In Scandinavian myth we have Freya spinning her golden thread of destiny.

The sword on the bed? The sword resting. The sleeping sword waiting for its rightful owner. When Galahad takes it up he is taking up his destiny as knight of the Spirit Realms. The sword is action, will, power, energy. The long search is over; now is the time to act.

I have always felt uneasy with the symbol of the sword because I do not think killing one's fellow man is ever an act that can be justified. But if I take it to mean "his own spiritual dynamic – the spirit striking down through matter to express the spiritual will, in which it is similar to the Qabalistic concept of the Lightning Flash" (of God's will that vitalizes the whole tree), as Gareth Knight does in his book *The Secret Tradition in Arthurian Legend*, or as "the penetrating power of the intellect", spiritual decisiveness and the defender of the sacred, possessing supernatural powers when wielded by the Solar Hero, "conqueror of dragons and demonic powers", as J. C. Cooper does in *An Illustrated Encyclopaedia of Traditional Symbols*, I am happier with it.Even St Paul talks about "the sword of the Spirit, which is the word of God" (Ephesians 6:17).

Why was the first sword, drawn from the stone, abandoned in favour of the new one? Is it because they represent different stages in the initiation of Galahad?

Why the pommel of multi-coloured crystal? J. C. Cooper points out that in Celtic mythology "the sword is the active aspect of the will, with the crystal as the passive". In Japanese mythology there are three particular treasures: the sword, courage and strength; the mirror, compassion; and the jewel or crystal, truth.

The sword is held in readiness by the Solar Hero, the crystal pommel "containing" the readiness, guarding against rash use, and guarding the hand of the wielder from harm. The crystal in this sense suggests that the wielder of the sword is in control. He knows when to strike and when not to. The power and energy are latent, quiescent. Without the crystal of truth, and clarity of vision, the sword is not a spiritual force, but a dangerous weapon. That is why Solomon had to remove the old pommel and replace it with this one.

Why is it made of so many coloured crystals and why must they appear as though they are one crystal? The world is full of disparate elements ('colours'), but when they are as "one" they are most effective. The guard around the hero's hand, that which protects him from the misuse of the sword, or of damaging himself with it, is the conception he has of the "wholeness", the interdependence, of all things.

Why are the ribs on the hilt made of those particular bones? Solomon, centuries before, had used the bones of two creatures: one from the earth and one from the ocean. The serpent here I think represents the power of the earth (the body), while the fish represents the power of the ocean (the spirit). The one gives control over the body so that one can no longer feel heat. The other gives control over the will so that one's spiritual powers become marvellously concentrated. One is from the far, cold north (Scotland); one from the hot Middle East. The suggestion is that the power contained in the sword is drawn from far and wide. The Hero will be a man of all nations.

That the scabbard is of snakeskin suggests again that the power in repose is of the earth, but when it is drawn in the hand of the Solar Hero it is the flash of the spirit that we see.

In myth swords are named, swords speak, swords dictate who shall use them and who shall not. The name of the sword that Galahad finds is "Sword of the Strange Belt". Why are there two belts – both so strange yet so different? The first, of hemp, lies on the bed dormant for thousands of years. The sword does not need a strong belt because in all that time it is not going to be used. The second is fashioned of gold and precious stones, and most important of all the sacrificed hair of the young woman. Galahad would not have found the sword if she had not led him to it, and he would not have been able to wear it and use it if she hadn't made the belt. She arms him, as a Celtic mother would her son entering manhood. She is his Higher Self. The golden princess of so many legends, now a bride of Christ.

In myth hair is of great importance. We remember Samson, who could not be defeated unless his hair was cut. We remember Rapunzel, whose long plaits acted as a rope ladder for her rescuer. We remember the shaved heads of the collaborators in Paris after the war. We remember the furore in the 1960s when young boys and men tried to assert their independence from the "establishment" by growing their hair long. We remember that the first thing the army does to a recruit to remove his individuality from him is to cut his hair.

The young maiden in this story cuts off her hair to signify acceptance of a role she has been given. She weaves it into a belt of power to aid the Solar Hero in his mission. "The hair is the expression in physical terms, of the emanations of the head centres, in terms of the human aura" (Gareth Knight).

In the belt, the crystals that are fused together in the pommel are separate. They have their separate powers, known to Solomon. The sword is not in use when it is hanging from the belt. But when the Hero draws it the powers work together, and must work together. They must be united as one power in his hand.

Sources

The Quest of the Holy Grail, translated by P. M. Matarasso from a medieval manuscript (Penguin Books, 1969).

Sir Thomas Malory, *Le Morte D'Arthur*, 2 vols, edited by Janet Cowen (Penguin Books, 1969).

Gareth Knight, *The Secret Tradition in Arthurian Legend* (Aquarian Press, 1983).

J. C. Cooper, *An Illustrated Encyclopaedia of Traditional Symbols* (Thames & Hudson, 1978).

Chapter 6

The Two Swords of King Arthur

(Western Europe: Arthurian)

One: The Sword in the Stone

At the death of Uther Pendragon the country was in turmoil. He had left no heir, and many strong barons competed for the throne.

Merlin, the Druid, the great sage-enchanter of the age, persuaded the Archbishop of Canterbury to call all lords of the realm to London, there to witness some extraordinary marvel on the birthday of Christ. It was understood this marvel would indicate Uther's heir.

As the lords gathered from far and wide they were amazed to see, in the churchyard of the church in which they were about to celebrate High Mass, an anvil in a block of stone. And held fast within it was a sword engraved with these words: "Whosoever draws this sword from here was born the rightful king of Britain."

Many tried to draw the sword, but all failed. The archbishop, believing that the king would be found by this means, arranged a programme of tournaments and feasts to keep everyone together.

And so it chanced that Sir Hector brought his son Sir Kay and his young foster-son Arthur to the festivities. Sir Kay had only just been knighted and was anxious to try his skill at jousting, but found that he had left his sword at his father's lodging. He sent Arthur running back for it. When Arthur arrived the lodging house was shut up as everyone had gone to watch the tournament, so Arthur, keen that his brother should have his chance at the joust, ran to the churchyard and pulled out the sword that was stuck in the stone, and took it to his brother.

Then, of course, there was great excitement and confusion. Most of the lords were angry that a young boy with no royal blood in his veins should rule over them. Time and again Arthur showed how he could put back the sword and draw it out again while no one else could, and Sir Hector revealed how Arthur had been brought to him by Merlin as an infant and was not his natural-born son.

Comment

That there are two stories in the same cycle of legends about a sword being drawn out of a stone might indicate the confused and rambling nature of the legends, or it might indicate that a good symbol is by no means weakened by being used more than once. Both Galahad and Arthur have been marked for an important destiny. They live quiet and blameless lives until such time as they are required to take up the sword – the blazing shaft of spiritual energy that only they are capable of wielding – because of blood, because of Divine Will, and because they are potentially very great men.

The moment is right. They seize it – and they are transformed.

As the whole cycle of legends unfolds we are drawn to consider that the themes of Galahad and Arthur are somehow part of a counterpointing system. It is not by accident that the incidents of the swords echo each other. Galahad is the totally spiritual man, completely pure. Arthur is a great man, strong and wise, but very human and subject to the confusions of the flesh.

They are given the same task and we watch how they each carry it out.

Two: Excalibur

One day Arthur and Merlin came upon a rich pavilion beside a fountain, and in it they found a fully armed knight seated in a chair.

"Sir knight," Arthur said, "why are you sitting here? Are you waiting for someone to come by and joust with you? That is an old custom and should be abandoned."

"Make me abandon it," Sir Pellinor replied belligerently.

"I will!" cried Arthur, and without more ado they fell to battle.

In the fight Arthur's sword was smashed into two pieces and he all but lost his life. In fact, if Merlin had not stepped in and put an enchanted sleep upon Sir Pellinor, Arthur would have been slain.

Arthur was taken to a hermit's hut where he abode three days. At the end of that time his wounds were healed and he was ready to ride – but he had no sword. Merlin told him that his sword was nearby.

Puzzled, Arthur rode with him until they reached a lake. It lay before them like a broad sheet of silver, and from the water rose an arm, clothed in white samite, holding a sword on high.

Approaching them they saw a beautiful woman walking on the water.

"She is the Lady of the Lake," whispered Merlin. "Speak fair with her and she will give you the sword."

Arthur spoke fair, and the Lady of the Lake said the sword Excalibur would be his if, when she asked it, he would give her a gift. He vowed at once to do so and she indicated a boat drawn up on the shore. Arthur rowed out to the sword and took it. As he did so the arm withdrew beneath the water. Nothing could be seen but the quiet rippling of silver, and in his hand he held a sword more magnificent than he had ever seen, "the pommel and the haft all of precious stones' (Sir Thomas Malory, *Le Morte d'Arthur*, Vol. 1, p. 516).

Some time after this King Arthur was in his court with all his knights around him when a young damsel entered wearing a sword at her side. She claimed that she wanted to rid herself of it, but could not. Only a knight of absolute purity would be able to take it from her. Needless to say Arthur and many of his knights tried to do so – but all failed. At last a poor and disregarded knight called Balin took hold of it and held it in his hand. The damsel warned him it would bring about his destruction, but he insisted on keeping it as he had no sword of his own.

At this moment Balin, seeing the Lady of the Lake and recognizing her as the evil enchantress who had brought about his mother's death, smote off her head with the very sword he had just won from the damsel.

Arthur was furious, saying that he was indebted to the lady.

Balin fled the court pursued by a knight seeking vengeance on Arthur's behalf.

When Merlin was old and foresaw his own end, he warned Arthur to guard Excalibur and its scabbard well, for it would be stolen by a woman, and one whom Arthur trusted.

And so indeed it was, for his sister, Morgan le Fay, made a counterfeit and sent him into battle with it so that he would be killed. If it had not been for the magical interference of one of the Ladies of the Lake, Arthur would have been killed by Excalibur in the hands of Sir Accolan, Morgan's lover.

Later Morgan succeeded in stealing the scabbard, but not the sword. She flung it into a deep lake. It sank at once, for "it was heavy with gold and precious stones". She managed to avoid his pursuit by changing herself into a rock.

In the final battle of his life Arthur is mortally wounded by his traitor son, Mordred, conceived in incest on his sister Morgan. As he dies he charges Sir Bedivere to throw Excalibur into the lake.

Bedivere sets off for the lake and raises the sword to throw it in the water, but...

the haft twinkled with diamond sparks,
Myriads of topaz-lights, and jacinth-work
Of subtlest jewellery. He gazed so long
that both his eyes were dazzled as he stood...

He cannot bring himself to throw it and returns to Arthur claiming that he has. Arthur asks him what he has seen, and what he has heard.

"I heard the ripple washing in the reeds,
And the wild water lapping on the crag."

Arthur is angry and demands that he go back and carry out his orders properly.

Bedivere returns to the lake and again is seduced by the "wonder of the hilt" so "curiously and strangely chased". He thinks it would be a wonder lost to future generations if he were to throw it away. Once more he returns to Arthur with a lie.

"What is it thou hast seen? or what hast heard?" the king asks, and Bedivere replies:

"I heard the water lapping on the crag,
And the long ripple washing in the reeds,"

Arthur accuses him of treachery and threatens to rise and kill him with his own hands if he omits once more to throw the sword into the lake.

Then quickly rose Sir Bedivere, and ran,
And, leaping down the ridges lightly, plunged
Among the bulrush beds, and clutch'd the sword,
And strongly wheel'd and threw it. The great brand
Made lightnings in the splendour of the moon,
And flashing round and round, and whirl'd in an arch,
Shot like a streamer of the northern morn,
Seen where the moving isles of winter shock
By night, with noises of the Northern Sea.
So flash'd and fell the brand Excalibur:

But ere he dipt the surface, rose an arm,
Clothed in white samite, mystic, wonderful,
And caught him by the hilt, and brandish'd him
Three times, and drew him under in the mere.

(Tennyson, "The Passing of Arthur')

When Bedivere tells Arthur this he knows Excalibur has been returned and is content to die.

Bedivere carries him to the lake shore, where a barge is waiting for him. Three queens dressed in black with golden crowns upon their heads take him aboard.

Bedivere watches as the barge glides out on to the lake and slowly disappears into the mist.

His heart is breaking. His king is dead.

Comment

Arthur loses the sword that he drew from the stone, the one that proved he was heir to the throne, when he enters a battle for no good reason other than that he wants to assert himself and show off his prowess. If Merlin had not been at hand to protect him he would have been killed and the great task he had been set would have come to nothing.

Arthur is a flawed hero, unlike Galahad. We get the impression that though he is a Chosen One he is sometimes not quite up to what is expected of him. He draws the sword from the stone without any sense of its significance and he loses it easily. He loses it because he has not yet grasped that it must be drawn only to defend right and defeat wrong.

He is given another chance – a more splendid sword – to mark the second stage of his initiation. This one is encrusted with crystals. We know by this that it is of great value. The crystals are clear gems representing clarity of vision, truth.

But even in receiving the sword he makes a foolish mistake (albeit one that many heroes in many legends make). He vows to give the enchantress any gift she might desire at any time she might request it. He cannot, in other words, see beyond his own nose. He cannot visualize a situation in which this could be a very dangerous vow indeed. He is trusting, to the point of stupidity. It is a wonder Merlin does not despair of him and find another king to support.

As we would expect she asks for a gift that he cannot honourably give.

Several times he is tricked by his sorceress sister, once to make love to her and father Mordred. As in the story of Oedipus, we wonder if he did not have some subconscious inkling that he was committing incest, and for this reason he had to pay: Oedipus pays with blindness and exile for making love to his mother, and Arthur pays with the betrayal of his wife and best friend, and the treachery of his son, for making love to his sister.

It seems Arthur never learns to be completely on his guard. Morgan steals Excalibur and uses it against him in the hand of her lover. Arthur is saved only by supernatural interference once again.

Later she strips him of Excalibur's magic scabbard, which is rich in protective jewels. Without it he is very vulnerable.

Alfred, Lord Tennyson's description of Excalibur in "The Coming of Arthur" is worth examination. "Excalibur," he writes,

> *...rich*
> *With jewels, elfin Urim, on the hilt,*
> *Bewildering heart and eye – the blade so bright*
> *That men are blinded by it – on one side,*
> *Graven in the oldest tongue of all this world,*
> *"Take me," but turn the blade and ye shall see,*
> *And written in the speech ye speak yourself,*
> *"Cast me away!"*

The "elfin Urim" harks back to the Bible (Exodus 28:15–2), where the Urim and Thummim are the precious stones in the high priest's breastplate, and of a miraculous nature.

It is interesting that the first message, "Take me," is in the oldest language of the world, as though Arthur's destiny has been set for him since the world began. He can read it because he is in a state of high visionary ecstasy. The command to give it back is in his own language. Why? Maybe because, by the time he has had the sword in his possession and his life has run its course, the sword knows (or whoever has given him the sword knows) that he would have failed to achieve the heights set for him and he would no longer understand the ancient script.

It is very sad that he has to trust one of his men to return the sword to its rightful place. He has to delegate a task he really ought to have performed himself. It was an important part of ancient Celtic religious ritual to return the hero's magic sword to the supernatural realms from whence it came.

Bedivere is tempted first by the richness of the jewel encrustment, and then by wanting to keep Excalibur as a marvel for other men to see. He does not understand that the sword is "spirit in action" and not only would it be a waste, but a danger, for it to lie idle. In the wrong hands such power could turn to evil.

I find it very interesting that the knights of the Round Table form a kind of club or group, a team if you like, and yet the real emphasis in the stories, particularly after a glimpse of the Grail set them off on the Great Quest, is always on the adventure, the trial, the heroism or otherwise of the individual. The Fellowship of the Round Table is part analogy for the world where we are members of a fellowship one with another, and yet on our own individual journey of exploration, undergoing our own personal trials to prepare us for the mysterious culmination we believe to be union with the Divinity from which diversity originally sprang.

As the *Zohar* implies, the 600,000 Israelites are together given the one revelation, but each interprets it according to his or her own stage of development and uses it according to his or her own personal destiny.

In these stories the use of crystal or precious stone (which is, of course, crystal) on chalice or sword marks the significance of the artefact. It is symbolic of the protagonist's effort towards discovering his or her Higher Self, and his or her journey, in the Higher Self, to the Higher Realms.

For those of us who think the mystique of the sword belongs only to ancient times I'd like to add here, almost irrelevantly, but not quite, a paragraph or two I read in a Far Eastern newspaper in 1987. It is a Reuter's report by Bill Tarrant from Imogiri, Indonesia. The headline is: "Keep an eye out for flying swords in Indonesia". The article begins:

> *Indonesia's traditional stabbing sword, the kris, rattles in its scabbard if it wants to be oiled and simply vanishes if it dislikes its owner...*
>
> *The wavy-bladed kris made by a master craftsman can also cure disease and keep its owner safe...*
>
> *Belief in the kris's mystical qualities is strongest in Java...*
>
> *To make a kris with power one first needs a handy meteor. Meteorite iron makes the best and most powerful swords...*
>
> *Nickel is used to create intricate patterns on the blade, which give each sword a unique character that is supposed to mesh mystically with its owner...*
>
> *The more elaborate scabbards are studded with diamonds, rubies and sapphires with intricately carved hilts of ivory or teak. The blades are sometimes inlaid with gold and can have up to 31 curves...*
>
> *...a kris will rattle if it wants to be cleaned or if it senses danger...It happens from time to time in the museum...*
>
> *Stories about magic kris may seem preposterous to westerners but highly-educated Indonesians, maintain considerable respect for the strange weapon and warn skeptical foreigners not to treat them lightly.*

The day I read this article I was also reading J. F. Campbell's *Popular Tales of the West Highlands*. My eye fell on the following passage (Vol. I, p. lxvii). The magic sword in legend "shines, it cries out – the lives of men are bound up with it. In one story a fox changes himself into the sword of light, and the edge of the real sword being turned towards a wicked "muime", turned all her spells back upon herself and she fell a withered faggot."

Soon after I found a picture of a sword embedded in a stone in J. G. MacQueen's book on the Hittites. It was a picture of a carving in the ancient Hittite Sanctuary of the Gods near Hattusas (present-day Yazilikaya near Bogazkoy in Turkey). An ancient Hittite text from the second millennium before Christ describes a priest making images of the gods in the shape of swords and fixing them in the ground.

There seems to be no beginning and no end to the resonance of a symbol.

Sources

Sir Thomas Malory, *Le Morte d'Arthur*, 2 vols, edited by Janet Cowen (Penguin Books, 1969).

The Quest of the Holy Grail translated by P. M . Matarasso (Penguin Books, 1969).

Alfred, Lord Tennyson, *Idylls of the King* (Macmillan & Co., 1958).

J.K. Campbell, *Popular Tales of the West Highlands* (1860; my edition Wildwood House, 1983), Vol. 1, p. lxvii.

J.G. MacQueen, *The Hittites and their Contemporaries in Asia Minor* (Thames & Hudson, 1975, 1986), pp.129–30.

Chapter 7

The Crystal Palace

(Western Europe: Brittany)

There once lived a poor couple who had seven children. The youngest boy, Yvon, and the only girl, Yvonne, were considered to be simpletons by the rest of the family and were the butts of many a harsh joke.

One day when she was minding her father's flocks and herds, Yvonne was approached by a beautiful young man who asked her if she would marry him. Startled, she asked for time to think about it and they arranged to meet the following day. She told her family and they seemed indifferent as to whether she went away or stayed, so she agreed to marry the young man. The wedding was very grand, and at the end of the ceremony she rode away with her new husband in a golden coach. On enquiring where they would be able to find their sister in the future the bridegroom replied: "At the Crystal Palace, on the other side of the Black Sea."

After a year had passed her brothers decided to visit her. Five of them set off, leaving the sixth, Yvon, to do the chores.

They rode a long way towards the east, constantly enquiring for directions to the Crystal Palace, but no one seemed to have heard of it. One day they came to a huge, dark forest, so thick it seemed impassable. A woodman, however, told them about a path and they set off. At one point a storm lashed the treetops so fiercely they nearly turned back, but when it passed they rode on.

As night approached they became more and more afraid, until they spotted a fire and hurried towards it. Once more a storm howled through the branches of the trees, and ceased as suddenly as it had arisen.

Beside the fire they found an old bearded hag. When they asked directions to the Crystal Palace she acknowledged at once that she knew the place and said she would ask her eldest son to guide them at least part of the way there.

Suddenly they heard thunder again, and livid lightning flashed through the darkness.

"Quick. Hide yourselves," the old woman said. "It is my son."

They hid in some bushes at once, and trembled to see the size of the giant who strode into the clearing. The giant, sniffing the air, at once demanded human flesh for his supper. The old hag took out a huge cudgel and threatened him with dire punishment if he dared to harm his cousins who had come to visit.

The giant seemed afraid of the old hag and agreed to let them be. He also agreed to set them on their way to the Crystal Palace.

At midnight he declared it was time to set off and laid a large black sheet on the ground, telling them to get on to it mounted on their horses. When this was done the giant stepped into the fire and within moments had become an enormous burning ball that rose into the air, the brothers on the black sheet floating up beside it like a cinder. They travelled this way for some time but eventually came down on a huge plain. The strange thing about the plain was that half of it was desert and on this half fat and healthy horses roamed about, and the other half was rich and fertile land on which the horses were thin and scrawny and fighting each other for every mouthful.

The giant left them at this point. Finding that their own horses had died on touching down on the plain, the brothers tried to catch some of the other horses – but to no avail.

At last they decided they could not bear it any more and turned for home.

On their return without having seen their sister, Yvon announced that he would find her, come what may. They laughed at him, of course, but this did not deter him.

He set off towards the rising sun and came at last to the dark, deep forest his brothers had found. There a pleasant old woman gave him directions to the Crystal Palace, charging him that no matter how many things frightened him on the way he must keep going courageously. She mentioned a road of black earth that he must follow beyond the plain.

He thanked her warmly and set off.

All went well until he reached the black road, and there he hesitated because it was writhing with venomous serpents. Remembering the old woman's instructions, he tried to drive his equally frightened horse forward. In a very short while it was bitten and died, leaving him on foot. Frightened, but courageous, he walked forward and came to the end of the road unharmed.

Now he found himself on the shores of a lake so huge that he could not walk round it. There was no boat and he could not swim, but he knew that he had somehow to cross it. He stepped into the water and walked steadily forward, persisting even when the water was over his head.

At the other side he found himself on a path overgrown with thorns so sharp that at the end of it his flesh was torn and bleeding. Nevertheless he made his way through it.

Exhausted, he was delighted to find his horse, which he had thought dead, waiting for him. He mounted thankfully and rode until he came to a place where a large slab of stone was seen to be resting on two others. A voice commanded him to dismount and enter the tunnel that lay between them. This he did and he found himself immediately in a dark and noisome place. He struggled forward trying to ignore the horrible smell and the fearful sounds of demons screeching and howling at his heels. Thankfully, at last, he glimpsed light at the end of the tunnel and hurried towards it.

Outside he was faced by a choice of roads. He chose the one that went straight ahead and found himself having to climb over a series of firmly locked gates.

At last he saw before him a sight that lifted his spirits. A shining crystal palace rose out of a crystal plain. Every thing shimmered and glimmered with light. He had found what he had been seeking.

Running at once to the crystal buildings, he found to his disappointment that not one of the doors could be opened. He circled for a while trying each one and then had the idea of squeezing himself through a small ventilation shaft into the basement. From there he made his way up into the building and wandered about till he found his sister asleep on a couch.

She had been transformed into a shining and beautiful woman. To reach her he had passed through halls of increasing light and beauty. Awed, he stood and gazed at her but did not attempt to wake her.

At nightfall her husband entered, gave her three blows, and lay down beside her. In the morning he gave her three more blows and left. She slept on peacefully.

Yvon stooped down and kissed her, and at once she awoke and was delighted to see him. They spent a few happy days together, the young woman denying that her husband gave her blows night and morning.

"You are wrong, brother," she said. "My husband gives me three kisses night and morning."

She also seemed unperturbed that her husband disappeared every day and she had no idea where he went.

Yvon asked her husband if he could accompany him one day and the husband at once agreed, but only on condition that Yvon would not touch anything and would speak to no one but himself.

The young man promised, and they set off.

At one point they passed a desert plain where fat, healthy cattle chewed the cud, and a fertile valley where thin, emaciated cattle fought each other for each blade of grass. Puzzled, Yvon asked his brother-in-law about this anomaly and was told that the fat cattle were poor but contented people, while the thin and quarrelsome cattle were rich, greedy, and dissatisfied people.

Later they passed two trees apparently fighting so fiercely against each other that their branches were splintering and breaking off. Yvon chided them and told them to live in peace. At once the spell was broken and the two trees became two humans, a husband and wife who had been so quarrelsome in life they had been doomed to fight like this until released by some caring passer-by. Now they were free to travel on to Paradise.

Yvon's brother-in-law now told him he had to return to the palace because he had broken his vow not to talk to anyone or anything. He promised to return himself later and show him the way home.

They parted in a friendly fashion, and the brother-in-law assured him he would not have as hard a time going back as he had in coming. He also promised him that he would soon be back in the beautiful Crystal Palace with his sister, so he must not be sad to leave now.

The journey was quick and easy and Yvon was soon back where he believed his home to be. The only trouble was, it was no longer there, and everyone he asked denied ever having heard of his family. He found their graves in the churchyard and realized he had been gone a long, long time.

Comment

This must surely be a story about the difficult journey of the soul towards awareness of the Higher Self and union with the Deity.

Christ said: "Suffer little children to come unto me for of such is the kingdom of heaven" (Luke 18:16), and we note in this story that it is only the two who are thought to be simpletons by the others who actually reach the Crystal Palace.

That the palace is made of crystal with transparent walls suggests that in this Otherworld nothing is hidden, all is revealed. "For now we see through a glass, darkly; but then face to face." But even so there are some mysteries beyond our comprehension. Where does the prince go each day? The ways of the Deity are still a mystery and can only be revealed to someone with a pure heart *and* absolute obedience – qualities that do not come easily to the human being.

The two, Yvonne and Yvon, came to the Crystal Palace in different ways. Yvonne was chosen and rode in a golden coach. Yvon was drawn there by his love for his sister and came the hard way, passing difficult tests and facing many dangers. The brothers never reached it because they came out of curiosity and had never shown any love or care for their sister until they thought she might be rich.

To the true "bride of Christ" blows seem like kisses. The hardships of this life are interpreted as loving tests, the passing of which bring great rewards.

The meeting with the fearsome giant who shows the way is a common theme in myth. The faint-hearted can make no progress on the road. The giant has to be overcome or tamed in some way – in this case, with the help of his mother.

In Dr Derek Bryce's able commentary on the story he equates the old hag with the Earth Mother, and the giant with the fearsome, scorching aspect of the sun; the bridegroom being the healing, life-giving aspect of the sun. Dr Bryce points out that this tale obviously predates Christianity in its sun-worshipping aspects.

The Crystal Palace is the Otherworld (the Am-Duat of the ancient Egyptians) – the place where the sun goes at night, the place where all go to await rebirth at the dawning of a new "day".

Even in very ancient sun-worshipping times the sun-god was never literally the sun as we see it in the sky. It was a powerful symbol for the spiritual illumination humans sometimes experience but can never explain except by analogy with the sun, the source of light on this earth. The Christians did not have to alter the ancient pagan stories too drastically to make them mean what they wanted them to mean; a universal wisdom was already implicit suitable for both pagan and Christian.

That the giant represents the fiery, scorching aspect of the sun does not preclude him also representing symbolically the fearsome aspect of Jehovah in the Old Testament in contrast to the strong but forgiving aspect of the Deity, the Christ (the golden prince married to Yvonne).

The old hag – the old Goddess-orientated religion – modifies the worst aspects of the male-orientated religion so that the pilgrim can go forward and find his way. But even this modified religion cannot take you the whole way. You yourself must have the will and courage to persist. The old religions, female and male-orientated, even united, can just point you in the right direction.

I think Bryce is right in equating black with mystery. We often find this in legends. The brothers were wrapped in a black sheet and carried blind into the Unknown. Their steeds were taken from them. They were alone, facing the unknown, on foot. They gave up.

It is interesting that Yvon meets the old woman and she does not appear ugly and bearded to him. There is no mention of the giant and she gives him instructions for the way herself. Perhaps Yvon, being so pure of heart, does not need the intermediate state represented by the giant. Yvon saw the old matriarchal religion as a kindly old woman. He progressed without having to go through the dangerous and violent history of male-orientated religion. The old matriarchal religion was ugly to the brothers, but they needed its help. The old patriarchal religion was frightening to the brothers, but they needed its help. Both could take them some of the way, but ultimately it was up to them – and they failed. Yvon succeeded, but only after overcoming some formidable dangers and steadfastly keeping to the path the old woman had indicated.

The various dangers he has to face are all highly symbolic. The road of snakes may well represent the dark and chthonic powers of the earth; the strong and disturbing sexual drive. The water of the great lake represents purification. Long before the Christians took it for baptism, initiates and priests plunged into sacred lakes to wash off the taint of their former lives. The path of thorns and brambles that tear at his skin suggests the sufferings that hermits and monks induce to purge the soul of the last vestiges of pride, lethargy, and greed.

Having come through all this he is given his horse back, the horse that had been dead. He is waiting for him at the entrance of the Otherworld. The helper (the horse) he had used at the beginning of his journey, was taken away from him in the middle, because he had to pass all the trials by his own unaided effort. Near the end he is allowed to have his original helper back, but in a transformed state, capable of carrying him into the spirit world.

The tunnel Yvon has to pass through to reach the Otherworld is reminiscent of the tunnel so many people describe when they have near-death experiences.

But even after the tunnel the way is not clear. We are faced with a choice of paths. Who knows to what terrible place the wrong one will lead us? The right one, the straight one, the one stretching ahead, the difficult one, will lead us to our Higher Self. But even on this path there are gates which we have to negotiate with skill and ingenuity. After death the ancient Egyptians believed in a series of gates that had to be passed through before one reached the Judgement Hall of Osiris, the god of resurrection and renewal.

Finally Yvon passes all tests with his pure and loving heart, his simple faith, and true obedience. He reaches the land of crystal and the Crystal Palace blazing with light. But there are no doors that open to him. Even here he has to use his intelligence and his steadfast determination to penetrate into the heart of it. He enters through a ventilation shaft and the basement like a burglar. Why is he not welcomed at the front door after all that he has won through? Perhaps because he still has not passed all the tests. The final one – the one of complete and unquestioning obedience – is still to come and he does not pass it. This is the most difficult of all. By releasing the two trees he questions the justice and the judgement of God.

Dr Bryce suggests that the Black Sea is not a geographical location at all, but a symbol for the mystery through which they have to pass to reach the Shining Crystal Land. In Christian terms it is "the dark night of the soul". I agree with this, but think that we also ought to take into consideration that on another level it might be harking back to an ancient race memory. Many scholars believe that the Celts of Brittany (Armorica) came originally from the countries bordering the Black Sea. Even today in countries like Georgia, the ancient Celtic legends are still alive and respected.

Dr Bryce in his introduction to his translation of the story says many important things, one of which is that "truly great or inspired literature is characterised by two things: Its use of language, and the plurality of meanings contained in one and the same piece of writing. These old legends can be regarded as great by virtue of the variety of meanings contained in them." Luzel wrote these Breton legends down in the 1860s and the 1870s from the oral tradition in Brittany. Many of them predate Christianity, but have been altered to accommodate Christianity. Some scholars find this reprehensible, but I do not. I believe that, rather than being altered, certain truths already within them have been drawn out. It has ever been in the nature of legends to lend themselves to many different interpretations and to adapt superficially to the time and place of the telling, while keeping the deep and universal truths they contain unchanged and unspoiled. That is their great strength.

Source

Celtic Folk-Tales from Armorica, written down in the 1860s and 1870s by F. M. Luzel, and translated, with an introduction and commentaries, by Dr Derek Bryce (Llanerch Enterprises, Wales, 1985).

Chapter 8

Princess Velandinenn and the Diamond Ring

(Western Europe: Brittany)

Three brothers were out hunting in the forest. They saw an old woman fill her water jug at a spring and then walk off with it balanced on her head. The eldest brother, Cado, thought it would be amusing if he shot the water pot off the old woman's head. In spite of the protests of his brothers he took aim and the old woman was soused with water. She looked at him angrily and promised him that he would pay for what he had done. He found himself shaking uncontrollably and she told him he would not be cured of this malady by anyone but the Princess Velandinenn.

The brothers returned home and told their father about what had happened. He shook his head at the foolishness of his eldest son and suggested that he should set off at once in search of the mysterious princess. No one knew where she was to be found but Cado's father suggested he should ask his uncle, a hermit living in the forest. The young man set off carrying a letter from his father to his brother, the hermit.

The hermit broke off his prayers to attend to the young man and searched through his books to see if he could find out any information about the princess. While he was waiting Cado chewed on a dry crust.

His uncle could not help him, but gave him a letter for another hermit living a long way away, deeper in the forest. He also gave him an ivory ball which he said would roll through the forest and guide him to his second uncle, the second hermit.

The second hermit, though he could communicate with all

the creatures of the forest, could not tell Cado where to find the princess. He blew a silver whistle and flocks of birds came to him. None of them knew where the princess was. At last the eagle arrived and it was he only who knew where the princess was. He was prepared to carry Cado on his back to find her if he were kept well supplied with food. Cado's uncle loaded meat on the eagle's back and Cado sat on top.

While they were flying, the eagle prepared Cado for what he would be seeing. "The castle where the princess lives is on an island surrounded by sea. On the shore is a spring of fresh water beneath a tree with overhanging branches. Every noon the princess goes to the pool with her handmaid. She sits combing her hair and gazing at her reflection in the water. She will make you welcome and heal you of your malady, but in exchange you will help her to escape from the wicked magician who is her father. I will be waiting to carry you back to our homeland."

Throughout the journey the eagle demanded food and ate it hungrily.

They arrived at the island eventually and Cado saw the princess as the eagle had foretold. She was as beautiful as the sun. As he stepped forward from the bush behind which he had been hiding she saw his reflection in the pool, beside hers. She turned to him at once, apparently knowing all about him and how he had treated the old woman and been punished in return. She gathered flowers and herbs and made a healing salve which she applied to his limbs. Soon his shaking stopped and he was healthy again. She told him about her father, and they planned their escape the following noon while he was asleep and after they had prepared enough food for the eagle on the return journey.

When the old magician found that his daughter had fled he pursued her at once on a dromedary, and because this beast was a magical one he began to gain on them. The princess dropped a little of the salve she had prepared for Cado into a river they were flying over, and the river at once overflowed its banks and made a lake so wide the father could not cross it. He tried to drink it up – but it was too much for him and he died.

The young couple believed they were safe, but the eagle began to weaken for lack of food. Cado cut a piece off himself to feed it, and again later he had to do the same thing. It was only because of this that they eventually reached the hermit's hut. Cado seemed on the point of death, but the princess managed to heal him. After they had rested and recovered they were sent on their way to the hermit's brother with a letter. Here again they were refreshed after their travels and given a letter for Cado's father. The princess and Cado were very much in love, but she refused to come straight to his father's house and be married to him. She built herself a house in the forest, and said she would wait there for him to come and fetch her. In token of their love she gave him a diamond ring. She charged him to wear it and never part with it.

Excitedly he returned to his family. Within a very short time Cado's sister had wheedled the ring off his finger, and as soon as it was off he forgot the princess instantly.

One day the three brothers were again hunting in the forest and they came upon a beautiful shining palace. They gained entrance to it on the pretext of asking for a drink after the exhaustion of hunting.

The Princess Velandinenn was their hostess but Cado did not recognize her. She served them food and drink graciously and said nothing to Cado about their past relationship. The second brother found her most desirable and suggested an assignation. Smiling, she suggested they stay the night, and she told the second brother that he would have the room next to hers.

At midnight he went into her room, and the princess received him cordially but suggested he changed his shirt, providing him with an elegant silk one. Eagerly he put it on, but no sooner had he done this than the soft shirt became stiff and hard, and he found he had to spend the night trapped, unable to move. At dawn the shirt became soft again and he rushed back to his room. His brothers were most amused at his predicament, but agreed that they were in the presence of a magician and should get out of the palace as quickly as they could.

Time passed and Cado became engaged to a young woman he had known all his life. The wedding feast was prepared, and the youngest brother persuaded their father that it would be nice to invite the lonely princess who lived in the forest to the wedding. She accepted and on the wedding day rode up in a golden carriage. She was dressed in gold silk with diamonds glinting in her golden hair. No woman present could outshine her.

At the feast she sat next to Cado and he remarked on the magnificent diamond ring she wore on her finger.

"Try it on," she said quietly and slipped it on to his finger.

Instantly his memory of all that he had been through and what she had meant to him came rushing back.

The wedding celebrations were reorganized so that the second brother married the bride Cado now discarded, and the youngest brother married Princess Velandinnen's handmaid.

Comment

Here we have the theme of the three sons (or daughters) so common in legends. They represent three important aspects of the one human being.

The old woman they meet in the forest (another common theme in Celtic legend) represents the Earth Goddess in her old hag aspects. The Goddess in Celtic myth has always three manifestations: young maiden, mother, and old hag. She is in a forest, drawing water from a spring. This too emphasizes the Earth Goddess aspect.

Cado, the arrogant, thoughtless aspect of the young male, thinking only to show off, shoots an arrow at her water pot and humiliates her. He has no respect for the goddess. The better sides of his nature, his brothers, try to warn him, but he ignores them. The Goddess gives him a penance that will not be taken from him until he meets Princess Velandinenn, the young maiden aspect of herself, and this he cannot do until the completion of a long and arduous spiritual quest in which he will not only find her but his own Higher Self.

His father is the first one to give him advice on how to set off on the quest. The second help he gets is from his uncle, a hermit who, like the Earth Goddess, lives in a forest. The forest, as in so many legends, is the shadowy, mysterious region of the subconscious – the instinctive, "earthy" side of consciousness in which one gets back to one's basic nature, uncultivated and wild, unchanged by the conditioning of education and society. A hermit lives alone, in silence and meditation. He represents that part of oneself one contacts away from the hubbub of everyday life.

The first hermit consults his books. The first stage in such a quest is often book learning, but this is not enough: it helps one only part of the way. The young man is sent off to another hermit further along the "Path". His wisdom comes from communing with nature.

The ivory ball that rolls through the forest leading Cado to the second hermit probably represents the moon. The moon is strongly connected with the female aspect of the Goddess because it governs woman's menstrual cycles. The young man, so far advised by men, is led now by the deeper, intuitive, "feminine" side of his nature to where he needs to be for the next stage of his quest.

The second hermit cannot help the young man by himself. Not even the flocks of little birds that come at his call can help him. It is only the eagle, the highest-flying, most far-seeing of all creatures, that can. Note that the young man does not go direct to the eagle (the highest, most far-seeing part of himself). He has to work through the other aspects of himself before he can even catch a glimpse of the eagle. Even then it is not just a matter of climbing on its back and soaring away. He has to work hard to ensure that the eagle is constantly fed. Here I would say we are talking about the need to renew our spiritual strength constantly with nourishment from prayer, meditation, good works, learning...

The eagle describes how Cado will first see the princess, and all occurs as he predicts. One knows in advance or in theory what one should do or how one should be, but the knowing is not enough. One has to actively work through the training and personally experience the initiation.

An island in the middle of the sea suggests a place isolated from the ordinary consciousness and hurly-burly of everyday living. We are surrounded by the great ocean of consciousness.

On the shore there is a fountain or spring which represents the life-giving waters of the spirit that well up fresh and pure from the depths of the earth. Most legends give a very strong directive that "earth" and "spirit" are dependent on one another. They sustain one another, and whoever tries to ignore one at the expense of the other will suffer the consequences of imbalance.

Above this fountain is a tree with overhanging branches – the Tree of Life nourished by the waters of the spirit that spring from the depths of the earth (out of reach of the pollution humankind has brought to the earth).

At noon the princess and her hand-maiden sit by the spring. The princess combs her long golden hair and looks at her reflection in the pool. This is not a case of a young girl's vanity, but an indication that the burning reality of the Goddess (the Goddess is often represented by the sun in these ancient tales) can only be seen as a reflection. Her handmaid, the moon, does not look into the pool to see her reflection because her light is already a reflection of the sun's.

Note that when they first became aware of each other, it is their reflection they see. At this stage, as in Plato, the only reality we can recognize is the reflection, the shadow. The full blaze of spiritual reality is still too much for us.

The Higher Self is represented by the Sun Princess curing Cado of his malady – the malady which had been brought about by his own actions. She deems that he has suffered enough and tried hard enough to progress beyond that thoughtless, callous stage he was at before. She makes ointment from flowers and herbs nourished by the sacred spring. He is cured and they plan to go away together. It seems the princess is a prisoner of her father, an old magician. The only freedom she ever had was to come to the spring and comb her hair at noon when he was asleep. The princess represents the Higher Self – not God. The Higher Self is the prisoner of the Lower Self and can only escape when the sun (light) is at its highest and most powerful and she is beside the spring from which wells the spiritual energy that nourishes the Tree of Life.

They gather food for the eagle and set off on its back.

The father pursues them. Note that he is on a dromedary on the ground while they are flying high in the air. But to sustain their flight in the rarefied regions of the Higher Spiritual Realms is more difficult than for him to do so on the solid ground of the ordinary consciousness.

When the eagle runs out of food, Cado feeds it from his own body. We are reminded of those emaciated holy men who are so dedicated to the spiritual life that they sacrifice their own bodies, fasting beyond the point where it is safe to do so.

The eagle is weakening for lack of food, but due to Cado's sacrifices they manage to reach the hermit's hut, where they rest and are given food. To return to ordinary life having witnessed the splendour of the Higher Self is as difficult as the search for it has been. The eagle must be continually fed or we will lose what we have gained.

As they approach Cado's father's castle the princess gives Cado a diamond ring so that he will remember her. She believes he is not quite ready yet for complete union with her. He has to be tested back in his ordinary world to see if he has mastered all that he has learned on the quest. This is very important. How many people go to church or take courses on spiritual enlightenment and then go home and behave just as badly as they did before?

Cado is not ready. He is easily parted from his diamond ring (the symbol of his commitment to the Higher Self) and totally forgets about the princess and all she stands for. Even when he meets her face to face he does not recognize her and encourages his younger brother to make love to her. The princess appears to accept the brother, but it is obvious, when he is so easily tricked, that he is nowhere near being ready for her. Cado offers a lesser part of himself to her (his brother) – and is rejected.

I am reminded of people who glimpse something of the spiritual treasure that will transform their lives from the mundane to the divine, but so miscalculate the significance of it that they treat it no better than they would treat a casual love affair – returning to their old ways as soon as the moment is over.

The three brothers return to their father's castle, and Cado prepares to marry another woman. The wedding feast is set when the youngest brother suggests to the father that the princess they had met in the forest should be invited to the wedding. The youngest brother – the most innocent part of Cado – yearns to see the princess again, though he does not realize her full significance.

She arrives and so outshines everyone at the wedding that all are disturbed by her. Cado still doesn't recognize her but is drawn to her diamond ring. She gives it to him. He puts it on and instantly remembers.

This is the second diamond ring. The first ring was given as a test of fidelity – which he failed. This second one is given as a gift of "grace". He is forgiven for his human frailty and given the priceless gift of union with the inner goddess of light, his own illumined Self. He takes it with gratitude – at last realizing its true value. The lesser parts of his nature marry up with the lesser characters in the drama – but he himself is united with the source of light that he journeyed so far to find.

Looking at the two brides, he can distinguish between the greater and the lesser value, the greater and the lesser Self.

Source

"Princess Blondine" (in Breton, Princess Velandinenn), from *Celtic Folk-Tales from Armorica*, collected by F. M. Luzel in the 1860s and 1870s, and translated, with an introduction and commentaries, by Dr Derek Bryce (Llanerch Enterprises, Wales, 1985).

Chapter 9

The Crystal Cross of Glastonbury

(Western Europe: Arthurian)

A river divided the sacred ground of Avalon from the mundane world, and beside the bridge that spanned it a little chapel stood in Arthur's day. It was here the Grail seekers faced the last and most important test that decided whether they were to see the Grail or not.

The knights who arrived there were weary. They had fought lions and dragons, fearsome giants and hostile knights. They had endured the wilderness and survived the wiles of ladies. Many of them had grown old in the quest, and many had lost companions and friends on the way. They were now near the end of all their seeking. That mysterious Grail, the elusive emerald cup which no one had ever been able to describe properly, yet without which they believed they would never see God, lay tantalizingly ahead of them, housed at this time at Glastonbury – the glass island, where the barriers between the celestial and earthly realms were so often transparent.

Not much was known about the trial they were expected to undergo at this place, for of those who had been there before, some had gone insane and had spoken no word of sense since, some had met their deaths there, and some had gone on to higher matters and never told the world of their experiences. No doubt the wonders they had experienced after having come safely through the trials had wiped all memory of the horrors they had encountered from their minds.

Those that emerged unscarred and unchanged reported that they had fallen asleep and absolutely nothing had happened. They were loud in their condemnation of those who believed there was anything special or unusual about the chapel, and disillusioned about the whole quest.

"We've wasted our lives," they said, "looking for something that doesn't exist."

There is a story that one night King Arthur himself, resting from his travels at the nunnery on Wearyall Hill, was awakened from a deep sleep and found himself drawn towards the chapel. He arrived on foot without attendants, dressed as an ordinary man, full of excitement that he had been called to this place, and hope that it would mean that he would he privileged to see the emerald cup, the Grail, the Christ Chalice, containing the Light beyond all light.

The forest was thick almost up to the banks of the river, and full of shadows. The chapel, when he came upon it suddenly illumined by the moon, looked unexceptionable. It was hard to believe it was a place of such grave importance.

He stepped eagerly up to the door but, before he could touch it, it swung open, and the light that shone from its interior cast his shadow a long, long way behind him on the path.

He moved forward but found that he could go no further. There seemed to be a sheet of glass between him and the inside of the chapel, yet there was no glass there.

He stood on the outside looking in, wondering why he had been brought to the place if he was not to enter it, when he saw an aged priest at the altar, praying. Behind the altar was a small window.

Arthur had thought the chapel was light compare to the darkness of the forest that lay beside it, but as he glanced up at the window he saw a shaft of light pass through it and fall with blinding brilliance on the chalice the priest was holding in his hands.

Arthur shut his eyes against the glare, and when he opened them there was a young woman standing beside the priest with an infant on her hip. The king could see the child lift his hand to play with a strand of his mother's hair, while with the other he clutched at the crystal pendant that hung around his mother's neck. The woman was more beautiful than anyone Arthur had ever seen and seemed to be contained in a cocoon of light. With quiet and pleasant assurance she assisted the priest with the service of the Mass and at one point laid her babe down on the altar.

Arthur drew his hand across his eyes, puzzled as to whether he was really witnessing the incident or was dreaming.

When he looked again there was a figure lying on the altar, a man sacrificed and bleeding.

Arthur battered at the invisible barrier with his fists, calling out in horror at such a terrible sight.

The priest and the woman ignored him and continued to concentrate on what they were doing. It seemed to Arthur that the woman took something from the right hand of the sacrificed man and placed it on his chest. Another brilliant shaft of light burst through the window and fell on the large crystal Arthur could now see resting over his heart. The crystal concentrated the light in such a war that it seemed as if all the light in the world, and beyond it in the celestial regions, was blazing into it. Soon it was as though the altar was on fire and flames and smoke consumed both the man and the crystal. The shaft of light withdrew as swiftly as it had come, but in its place stood the risen Christ, the phoenix, born again from the fire of the Holy Spirit.

Then the Lady put her hand into the smouldering embers and plucked out the crystal unharmed. She turned to Arthur and began walking towards him, holding it out before her. With an expression of great love and compassion she presented it to him, and then he saw that it was in the shape of a cross. He put out his hand and took the gift, the barrier between them momentarily dissolved. As he gazed into it he knew that his life had reached a turning point. He had been too worldly to win a glimpse of the Grail, but the Queen of Heaven, the Mother of God, had given him a gift that would change his life forever.

He looked up to thank her, but she and her son were gone. The shaky old priest was fumbling to put the holy vessels away. The only light in the chapel was from the two altar candles and they were about to be snuffed out.

Arthur turned around and made his way thoughtfully back to Wearyall Hill through the forest. The first birds were beginning to sing. The first light from the sun was beginning to dawn.

In his hand he still held the crystal cross.

Comment

Arthur has always stood at the crossroads – the crossroads between history and legend, the crossroads between paganism and Christianity. Perhaps that is why he appeals to us so much. He is the past, yet it is foretold that he will rise again, so he is also the future. He is a great warrior, yet he is also a visionary who set his men to follow a spiritual quest. He has a highly developed soul, yet is not vouchsafed even a glimpse of the Mystic Grail.

In the ancient Welsh tales of the *Mabinogion* he is a pagan tribal chief riding with his men to face trial after initiative trial, culminating in the seizing of treasure protected between the mighty and fearsome tusks of the boar Twrch Trwyth, the comb, the razor, and the shears with which the giant Ysbaddaden is to be shaved in order that Arthur's nephew Culhwch shall win the giant's daughter Olwen to wife – the marriage won with such difficulty being no ordinary marriage, but, as so often in legend, symbolic of the man's union with his Higher Self.

According to Lady Flavia Anderson in her fascinating study *The Ancient Secret; Fire from the Sun*, Arthur was a Roman strongly influenced by the cult of Mithras, and his acceptance of the crystal cross from the Virgin Mary clinches his decision at last to accept Christianity. But even in this scene, apparently so heavily charged with Christian symbolism, the ancient religion has its part to play. Lady Flavia describes throughout her book how crystals were used in conjunction with the light of the sun to light sacred fires since very, very ancient times. The control of the power to make such fire was originally in the hands of pagan magician priests or priestesses, but later became the prerogative of the Pope, the cardinals, the bishops, who wore great crystals around their necks or on their fingers in subconscious memory of their ancient role as fire-makers for religious and sacrificial ceremonies.

Arthur saw how the sacrificial fire was lit around Christ by the pure light of Heaven from a crystal he, the Christ, carried in readiness, knowing his destiny. Like a proud Druid prince, perfect in mind and body, he voluntarily goes to his death to bring life back to a dead land and a lost people. The Earth Mother burns the fields with sacred fire to make way for the new growth.

The later medieval legends about Arthur make him a Christian king, and the cross he was given by Mary becomes the property of Glastonbury Abbey. John of Glastonbury in the late fourteenth century describes it as part of the treasure of Glastonbury and mentions that it is carried every Lent, on Wednesdays and Fridays, in procession by the monks. By the time Henry VIII looted the abbey it had disappeared, and Lady Flavia is of the opinion that it is still hidden in the grounds somewhere, the monks having determined that no heretic would touch it.

Geoffrey Ashe has pointed out in *King Arthur's Avalon* that the cult of Mary in Britain was very strong. He suggests it came mainly from the Byzantine Church via the Crusaders. Glastonbury certainly has always had a close connection with the Queen of Heaven, and her chapel in the abbey is the most numinous place still.

In a sense she has always been present in Avalon. There are legends of very ancient fertility rituals on the Tor and the release of the Earth Goddess, the Green Lady, from imprisonment within the Tor as the spring breaks through upon the land. The mythic female plays many important roles in legendary Glastonbury, from the powerful Lady of the Lake who lends Arthur Excalibur, his supernatural strength in the form of a sword sheathed in magical crystal talismans, through the mystical female guardians of the Holy Grail, to the numerous beautiful

maidens for whom the knights of the Round Table dare dangerous and impossible deeds and who, with almost no exception,
act as catalysts for transformation and bring about the knight's
discovery of his Higher Self.

Mary is in this tradition. She is the All-Mother, the Lady of
Sorrows, who has to bear the Saviour of the World and give
him up for the world.

Arthur is the World, the strong, physical world we see around
us, the world that struggles to be more than it is, but can only
reach beyond itself with help from above. Mary sympathizes
with his horror and his misunderstanding of the ritual he sees
enacted on the altar. No doubt she has wept and sorrowed sometimes when she should have accepted with confidence the
Mysteries of God. She holds out the crystal cross to Arthur –
the crystal lens that has conveyed the fire of Heaven (the Holy
Spirit) to earth to transform an ugly scene of suffering into one
with a positive purpose carrying hope for the future – the crystal that has always been used to light pure and sacred fire, but is
now shaped like a cross to carry a new and further charge of
meaning. The old religion transformed into the new. Note – not
discarded outright and vilified, but transformed.

Aquinas once said that the stone, the perfect crystal, is an
allegory for the soul of Mary, "ever the same and ever constant
and without flaw." The Light of God passes into her, through
her, and out again, causing her to conceive, yet without destroying her virginity.

The shamans of the so-called pagan religions kept crystals
in the precious paraphernalia of their craft, and not only to make
fire from the sunlight, but because they thought of crystal as
celestial light trapped in this form for use by the High Adept
and the Initiate. When someone was ill they believed his or her
soul had wandered off, and the crystal was used to seek it out
and bring it back to its rightful place. When a young man or
woman wanted to train as a shaman he or she underwent rigorous instruction on many matters, but the final and culminating
experience from which there was no going back, was to be symbolically cut open and have all internal organs replaced with

crystal. They believed that from that moment on they carried the Celestial and All-Seeing Light within themselves.

For Arthur who had undergone many things to bring himself to a state of near-enlightenment, the final symbolic act he needed to show his complete acceptance of the truths behind the new religion was to take this gift of sacred light. It is important that it is Mary who gives the crystal cross to Arthur – the same crystal she wore around her neck as the symbol of God's gift to her, his bride, to be passed on, after transformation by their son, to the world (Arthur).

Arthur now carries the Celestial and All-Seeing Light.

After his death Glastonbury Abbey carried it. It was seen and recorded by John of Glastonbury centuries later.

Where is it now?

It was not found by Henry VIII. And we certainly do not have it!

Sources

Dion Fortune, *Glastonbury, Avalon of the Heart* (1934; republished by Aquarian Press, 1986).

Lady Flavia Anderson, *The Ancient Secret: Fire from the Sun* (1953; republished by Rilko, 1987), p. 264.

John of Glastonbury, a monk, wrote a history of Glastonbury Abbey in the last half of the fourteenth century and mentioned this legend of the crystal cross.

Armine le S. Campbell, *The Glories of Glastonbury* (Sheed & Ward, 1926).

Geoffrey Ashe, *King Arthur's Avalon* (Fontana, 1957).

Chapter 10

Freya's Necklace, Brisingamen

(Northern Europe)

One day Freya, goddess of Love and Beauty, Queen of Heaven, lay sleeping on her couch, her arm resting on her long and shining necklace, Brisingamen. It had been fashioned deep in the earth by dwarfs from the rarest and most exquisite of crystals. It never left her, casting light to the furthest reaches of the universe.

At the gates of Asgard the watchman Riger held his post, his gaze sweeping over all who entered and who left, and all who moved within the twelve great palaces of the gods. His attention was drawn to Freya's chamber, and there he saw Loki creeping soft-footed to her side. Riger watched, for Loki, the giant, though as beautiful as any god, was full of tricks and guile and had been known to bring more evil in Asgard of the gods and Midgard of the mortals than any other.

He saw him reaching for the necklace, then drawing back his hand as he realized he could not pull it free without waking Freya. Riger thought of the danger if such a powerful artefact should fall into the hands of such a mischief-maker.

He saw Loki prowl about the couch in frustration. Then, suddenly, Loki turned himself into a flea and leapt upon the fine silver flesh of the goddess. He bit her on her side, and restlessly she turned in her sleep, freeing the necklace.

Instantly Loki was himself again, seized the radiant circle of gems, and made off with it.

Riger pursued him. Almost immediately he thought he had him and swung his sword, but as it touched Loki it seemed Loki was a pillar of fire and the sword passed right through him. Riger became a cloud and poured rain upon the fire to extinguish it. But Loki was now a polar bear that drank the rain. Immediately Riger was a larger bear pursuing Loki. He caught him and gripped him close. But Loki, as a seal, slithered from his deadly embrace.

Then Riger became a larger seal and they fought long and fiercely.

At last, wounded and weary, their seal skins fell from them and they faced each other in the forms of men, Riger's sword at Loki's throat. Pleading for mercy Loki flung the necklace at Riger's feet and fled.

Riger, panting and in pain, leant on his sword, holding the crystals limply in his left hand.

Iduna, the goddess of immortal youth, wife of Bragi, the divine poet, found him there. She drew one of her shining apples from the crystal dish where they were kept, and gave it to him to eat. No sooner had he tasted it than his wounds healed and youthful strength returned to his limbs.

"Iduna, lady of flowers and leaves, of burgeoning fields and forests," he said, "I entrust you with the necklace of Freya, the incomparable Brisingamen. Bring it to her and tell her the story of its loss and reclamation."

Freya listened quietly to the story told by Iduna and hung the shimmering jewels around her neck once more. The sun rose and all the world of mortals rose with it to go about its business.

Comment

In the Germanic creation myth, as it is told in the Edda, men were not created first. First there were the giants – then the gods who created the dwarfs... "only after having created innumerable dwarfs...did they create mankind" (Marie-Louise Von Franz, *Creation Myths*, p. 171). Von Franz sees the dwarfs of Germanic and Nordic myth as "preforms, the *not-yet* forms of human consciousness". "They represent the chaotic impulses from the unconscious which are not yet controlled by that continuous civilized form of consciousness for which the symbol of man stands..." They inhabit the dark and earthy regions of the sub-conscious and it is interesting that they are often described as magnificent craftsmen and artists. The dwarfs bring the jewels that are hidden deep in the subconscious and that would not otherwise be noticed by gods or men, to the attention of the so-called "higher" forms of being. They fashion magnificent and intricate artefacts out of these secret treasures – so exquisite that the gods and goddesses themselves desire them and promise many things to have them in their possession. It is said that Freya spent one night with each of the dwarfs who fashioned the necklace.

That Brisingamen, the necklace that shines like a thousand suns, is mined and fashioned by dwarfs is very instructive. Too often we forget that the real riches of existence are given us by instinctual, intuitive, "earth" consciousness and not by the scientific, rational consciousness. But only when the necklace is worn by a Being of Light does it come into its own. The gift of it to Freya by the dwarfs ensures a relationship of trust between them. The subconscious is honoured and protected by Freya because of the necklace. If it is destroyed that balance between the subconscious and the supraconscious will be destroyed, bringing in its wake many disasters.

Freya wears it as a token from the dark and destructive forces of the earth that they love her and will co-operate with her. She can function better as goddess because the unruly and rebellious forces of the earth have been transformed into something beautiful and helpful. They have not been suppressed or conquered, but transformed. She wears the necklace always to show that this transformation is always possible.

Loki tries to steal it – not for its beauty, but for its power. Riger knows that in the wrong hands the power of the subconscious can be very destructive.

In the chase of Riger and Loki we are not so conscious of the reincarnation, teaching, and rebirth elements, as we are in the story of Ceridwen and Taliesin, but of the struggle between two forces, one good and one evil, and the way this is acted out between inanimate elements (fire and water), between stronger and weaker animals, and between men. Though Riger and Loki are not mortal men they are in man-form during the last part of the fight. Riger is only returned to the World of the Immortals by the assistance of the goddess Iduna.

It is interesting that Riger does not return the necklace to Freya himself. His wit and strength win it back, but it is only a goddess who can safely handle it, and safely return it. It is only a goddess who understands its true significance and can control its power. When, centuries later, when Asgard is no more, and the necklace is given to Beowulf as a reward, he has it in his possession for a very short while before he gives it to the queen. This is not because males did not wear necklaces, because it is only recently that they have not – but the implication is that the feminine element in the male/female equation is the one that has struck the bargain with the dwarfs of the subconscious.

Loki resembles Lucifer in that he is a beautiful and great being to begin with, accepted among the gods, who later falls from grace and devotes his time to making mischief and creating discord and havoc. With the necklace he no doubt hoped to destroy the peace between the "dwarfs' and the "gods", and laugh at the mortals caught dangerously in the crossfire. In Celtic legend we have Bricriu playing the same role.

Sources

Asgard of the Gods: Tales and Traditions of our Northern Ancestors forming a complete manual of Norse Mythology, adapted from the work of Dr W. Wagner by M. W. Macdowall and edited by W. S. W. Anson (Swan Sonnenschein, Le Bas & Lowrey, London, 1886).

Marie Louise Von Franz, *Creation Myths* (Spring Publications, Dallas, Texas, 1983; UK distributor Element Books), p.171.

Chapter 11

Beowulf

(Northern Europe)

Overlooking the sea "where breakers beat at the headland" stood an ancient burial mound, the wind's companion. For three centuries it stood thus, undisturbed, until one day, running from an angry master, a frightened slave sought shelter on the headland. Squeezing into a cleft to hide himself he displaced some rocks and found the entrance to the hollow mound. He stood gazing in astonishment at what he saw. Gold gleamed in the dim light that now entered the place. The glint of crystal, the glow of precious jewels almost dazzled him. He had found the treasure hoard of a long dead people.

Beset as he was by fear of his master and terror of the ghosts that might be haunting the tomb, he darted forward, seized a golden goblet, and fled. He did not even notice in the shadows the long and menacing coils of a sleeping dragon.

To win back his master's favour the "luckless slave" gave him the golden cup.

Meanwhile the dragon woke and noticed that his lair had been entered and part of the precious treasure he was set to guard had been stolen. He issued forth wrathfully, armed with fire, intent on revenge. He devastated the land far and near, the king's own hall "swallowed in flame".

Then the great hero Beowulf roused himself. Half a century as king of the Geats had whitened his hair and stiffened his limbs since the great feat he had performed in fighting and defeating the monsters Grendel and Grendel's mother, but his people were in danger and he had to defend them.

A shield of iron was forged for him, and he set off with

eleven sturdy companions, led to the entrance of the burial mound by the miserable slave who had stolen the golden cup.

The sea crashed below on the rocks and the great king sat above the foaming water thinking back on his life, knowing that what he was about to do would probably bring about the end of it. Not for long would his life "be lapped in flesh". He remembered the long years of fighting for his ring-lord, the single-handed battle with the monsters of the lake that were night by night destroying the warriors of Hrothgar the Dane. He remembered the triumphs and the sorrows: his pride in receiving King Hygelac's most treasured sword, the heirloom of heroes, "Nageling", and his sorrow at the death of his uncle Hygelac, the generous sword-giver, gold-giver, friend. He remembered the nights in the feast-hall drinking ale from the great auroch horns, listening to the wild and beautiful tales of the word-spinners and the music of the harpers. He remembered wearing the richly jewelled necklace of Freya, the Queen of Heaven – his reward for the slaying of Grendel.

But now the years had passed and age was upon him, but gold at arm and throat still proclaimed him King, and as king he had a duty to save the land and his people. He spoke to his companions with courage and told them he alone would enter the mouth of the treasure cave.

He climbed to the entrance and stood before the stone archway. The fearsome beast within breathed fire and the whole place was dangerous with flame. Beowulf raised his voice and with a great cry challenged the enemy of his people. "The hoard-guard recognized a human voice" and his breath "billowed from the rock in a hissing gust; the ground boomed". The king "swung up his shield" to protect himself from the fire and gripped his "huge ancestral sword". The serpent came forward "flaming and coiling, rushing on its fate". The king brought down his blade on the creature's back, bending and buckling the tough metal. "The keeper of the barrow", wounded, flailed about in even greater rage, "spat death-fire" and enclosed the king in flame. In terror ten of his companions fled. One only, a young man called Wiglaf, Weoxstan's son, a kinsman, rushed to his side with no more protection than a shield of linden wood.

In the first onslaught his shield was reduced to ashes and he had to rely on his gold-lord to protect him with the iron shield. A third time the fire-drake attacked.

Desperately the two men fought the dragon, Beowulf this time sorely wounded, the fangs of the beast having sunk deep into his neck. But together they finally overpowered and slew him.

Mortally wounded, the king was carried from the place by the young warrior. Tenderly he bathed his wounds and ministered to him. The dying king made one last plea:

"Quickly go now,
beloved Wiglaf, and look upon the hoard
under the grey stone, now the serpent lies dead
sleeps rawly wounded, bereft of his treasure.
Make haste, that I may gaze upon that golden inheritance
that ancient wealth; that my eyes may behold
the clear skilful jewels..."

The young thane hurried back into the cave where the fire-drake lay dead – "the far-flyer felled" – and gazed with awe at the mounds of treasure. Taking what he could carry, he staggered back to his king and laid it before him. Beowulf gave thanks to his god that he had won this last great victory and left his people a worthy legacy.

He asked for his tomb to be built on a towering foreland by the sea

"that ocean travellers shall afterwards name it
Beowulf's barrow, bending in the distance
their masted ships through the mists upon the sea."

He gave the golden collar from his neck, the gold-plated helmet and heavy arm-ring, all his armour and his signs of kingship, to the young prince, then "attained the end of his life's lease".

Wiglaf sat beside his king in sorrow, but when the ten who had fled returned he stood up and with flashing eyes and bitter tongue berated them. The news was carried to the people and the burial prepared swiftly because Wiglaf could see that, with the powerful Beowulf dead, the Geats' old enemies might well attack the country.

The people, mourning, approached and the huge funeral pyre was made ready.

The winds lay still
as the heat of the fire's heart consumed
the house of bone.
    What remained from the fire
they cast a wall around, of workmanship
as fine as their wisest men could frame for it.
They placed in the tomb both the torques and the jewels,
all the magnificence that the men had earlier
taken from the hoard in hostile mood.
They left the earls' wealth in the earth's keeping,
the gold in the dirt. It dwells there yet,
of no more use to men than in ages before.

Comment

The earliest known manuscript of *Beowulf* dates from about AD1000, but there is no doubt that many elements in the story were part of the repertoire of storytellers many centuries before that. Michael Alexander in the introduction to his very readable version says that it is thought to have been the "product of a relatively sophisticated and Christian Anglian court – though one that had evidently not yet repudiated its ancestral links with the Germanic peoples across the North Sea", and many of the incidents are drawn from the adventures of the Age of Migration. But what makes it so great, and what makes it speak to us so loud and clear across the centuries, is the mythic content, the symbolism that links us all on the deepest level of our being. At the heart of this symbolism is the crystal, the precious stone, the hoard of treasure guarded by the fearsome beast that has to be defeated by the hero at great cost to himself.

We are dealing here with the climax, the apogee, of Beowulf's life. On the one level the story seems to be no more than the usual tale of a man facing danger heroically – and that, no doubt, would be enough for many of its hearers. But the treasure is not material wealth alone, nor the dragon physical danger. In one sense the dragon is the Unknown, the Darkness, the Chaos, the Void call it what you will – but it lies behind all things, and the treasure of life itself can only be won by facing up to it with courage. Before Beowulf enters the cave he sits beside the sea – often the symbol for the most profound consciousness. He knows what he will be doing when he faces the dragon.

In another sense Beowulf is performing an act of self-sacrifice for the good of his land and his people as the kings did in ancient times so that the spring might follow the winter. The treasure is buried with him – like seed.

At the same time he is arranging a test, an initiation, for the new leader of his people. Eleven of his best men are chosen to accompany him on his adventure, but only one proves in the end to be worthy of the challenge. Wiglaf shows he has enough initiative and courage to rule a nation, and Beowulf dies confident that his people are in good hands.

Before Beowulf dies he asks to see the treasure. He had not faced the dragon for the treasure. He had faced the dragon to save his people. But as "gold-giver" he is pleased he will have one last rich gift to give his thanes. That they choose to bury it with him rather than keep it for themselves shows that they understood by his sacrifice that there is something more to life than the acquisition of riches.

What is the significance of the slave stealing the cup? Have we an instance here again of the uninitiated "stealing" knowledge not meant for him, knowledge that is dangerous in the wrong hands? In this case we might suggest that the slave (the ignorant and unenlightened), not understanding the nature and significance of life or death, or the consequences of any of his actions, brings about a disastrous situation for everyone around him. Thinking only of himself, he steals the cup and causes more harm than good. The gift he presents to his master is presented with the wrong motive.

Another theme in this story that appears consistently in others is that Beowulf, a mortal, is called upon to defeat the dragon which has, up to this defeat, been immortal. In the Welsh legend the mortal prince Pwyll is called upon to change places for a year and a day with Arawn, king of the Otherworld, so that he, Pwyll, may defeat Arawn's immortal enemy Hafgan. Why can't Arawn, himself an immortal, defeat him? Again in the Irish story of Cuchulain, the mortal hero is called to do battle for an immortal to defeat an immortal. In the Scandinavian legend one of Olaf Tryggvason's men breaks into a tumulus and finds twelve men in black and twelve men in red fighting. As soon as they are killed they rise again. It is only the human who can deal them a blow from which they cannot recover.

Are these legends saying it is no good waiting until you are dead and in spirit form to defeat Evil? You have to do it while you are alive, in the flesh. *This* is the testing time. In *this* world you prove yourself worthy or not worthy.

Source

Beowulf, a verse translation by Michael Alexander (1973; Penguin, 1977).

Chapter 12

The Lake Maiden and the Carbuncle Ring

(Western Europe)

It was the beginning of May and the villagers of the Black Forest were celebrating. A maiden no one had seen before joined in the dance. She was dressed in green with river pearls encircling her hair and her neck. She was so beautiful all the young men vied with each other to dance with her, but it seemed she favoured only one, Michael by name.

As the village clock struck eleven she disappeared and no one saw her go.

The next night the celebrations continued and again she appeared, danced, and disappeared at eleven o'clock.

The third night Michael watched closely and followed her into the forest. He was hard put to it to find his way though he thought he knew the forest well. She led him down a path he had never seen before, and he caught up with her on the shore of a lake.

"Stay awhile," he cried, and she paused – though she looked anxiously at the moon-silver water as she did so.

He told her that he loved her and wanted to make her his wife. She shook her head saying that her father would never allow it. And then she stepped into the lake and disappeared.

Now he realized she was a lake spirit, but he still would not give up the idea of marrying her.

He waited the whole year to see her once more, and when she appeared at the May Festival he danced with her and again asked her to marry him. She said sadly that she could not, for her father would never consent to marriage with a mortal – but her father had sent him a gift. She slipped a ring with a huge carbuncle stone on to his finger.

"It will show you where all the treasure of the earth lies hidden," she said.

He held the ring out before him, and it seemed to him the earth had become transparent and he could see the veins of silver and gold and precious stones deep under the surface.

"I don't want the treasures of the earth," he said. "It is only you I want."

She sighed and shook her head and slipped away.

The next night he altered the village clock and danced with her long past the hour she usually disappeared. When the clock struck eleven she made for the lake as usual, with Michael close beside her. Suddenly they heard the clock of a neighbouring village strike twelve.

She was very frightened and ran in great agitation to the water's edge, Michael still beside her trying to persuade her to disobey her father and marry him.

"You have done a terrible thing," she told him. "My father has power over all the springs and wells and streams. If he is angry we will pay for it."

She told him that if white milky liquid welled up from the lake after she was gone he would know everything was all right, but if he saw blood he would know there was trouble.

She stepped in and where she disappeared an empty water funnel appeared. To his horror this soon filled up with blood.

In a rage he flung the carbuncle ring her father had given him against a rock and the crystal splintered into hundreds of pieces. The water seemed to boil and rise, and soon the lake had overflowed its shores and was flooding into the land. A great wave washed the young man away and drowned the village. Neither he nor the young maid in green was ever seen again.

Comment

The lake-father is not the only father who has tried to buy off a daughter's unsuitable lover and failed. His rage at the young lovers appears excessive, however, and the young man's rejection of the gem that would bring him X-ray vision and untold wealth should perhaps have softened the father's heart towards him.

If we look at the story from another angle, we can give it a different interpretation.

The young man rejects the gift Nature gives him – a means of gaining great insight and knowledge. He demands what Nature does not want him to have, and is persistent to the point of foolhardiness. He uses a trick to deceive the beings of the Otherworld, thinking only of himself and not for a moment considering that the young maiden (the balance of Nature) might be endangered by this thoughtless and selfish action. He understands nothing about her, and yet he wants to impose his own wishes on her. We are talking about those who try to impose their will on Nature without regard to its own well-being. In the twentieth century we know only too well what this leads to! We will be lucky if we have not already destroyed our planet. Hopefully it is still the eleventh hour, and not the twelfth.

His petulant flinging away of the ring, the gift he *was* given, because he could not have what he was not given, triggers real danger. The carbuncle ring probably stands for Nature's pledge that if you honour its laws you will have the true riches of the earth.

The fact that she had to abide by her father's rules so strictly, as shown by the careful observance of the curfew, and that disaster befalls when the young man tricks her into breaking those rules, emphasizes that the laws of Nature are not to be tampered with.

117

It is interesting that it is water – the most wonderful and life-giving of elements, and the one that most consistently symbolizes the higher consciousness in myths and legends – which is the element that becomes a destroyer when not respected.

Source

Asgard of the Gods: Tales and Traditions of our Northern Ancestors adapted from the work of Dr W. Wagner by M. W. Macdowall (Swan Sonnenschein, Le Bas & Lowrey, London, 1886).

Chapter 13

The Cow-herd and the Goddess Holda

(Western Europe)

There once lived a cow-herd in a remote valley of the Tyrol. He was a poor man with a wife and children to feed, and a small herd of cattle and goats to look after. He was a skilled bowman, and when he was watching the herd he carried a crossbow to protect them from the bears and wolves that roamed the mountains.

One day on one of the upland pastures he saw a magnificent chamois, its horns shining like the sun. He at once took hold of his bow and crept towards it until he was almost within range. The deer sprang from rock to rock, always just out of reach as he pursued it higher and higher up the mountain. From time to time it paused, looking back at him, almost as though it were challenging him to follow. He forgot everything else but the pursuit of this beautiful creature.

Eventually he found himself on a glacier among the permanent snows and ice. The chamois disappeared behind some huge boulders, and when the cow-herd followed it, it was nowhere to be seen. He found instead a huge arched cavity in the ice, and through it he glimpsed a strange and eerie light.

He was now too involved in the chase to turn back, and too curious to hesitate. He stepped forward through the arch and found himself in a huge hall, the walls and ceiling of which were pure and dazzling crystal decorated with huge garnets that glowed like flame. Through the transparent walls he could see meadows of sweet grass and leafy woods. In the centre of the hall stood a tall and beautiful woman, her garment shining like silver, her belt of gold. Her hair was the colour of the sun, encircled by a diadem of fiery carbuncle crystals. In her hand she held a sheaf of flowers as blue as her own eyes.

Trembling with awe, he fell down on his knees before her.

She smiled at him and spoke gently to him. She told him he could choose any of her treasures, silver, gold, or precious stones. Or, if he would prefer, he could have one of her hand-maidens. He could see them standing behind her. Apart from her, they were more beautiful than any women he had ever seen.

Humbly he asked only for what she held in her hand.

"You have chosen wisely," she said, and handed him the flowers. "You will live as long as these flowers bloom." She also gave him seeds and told him to sow the land with them.

He reached forward to touch her feet in gratitude, but the crystal hall shook with thunder and suddenly the vision was gone. He was on the icy mountainside, alone. Dazed, he rose to his feet and stared at the bunch of blue flowers in his hand and the wooden corn-measure of seed on the ground beside him. He picked it and himself up and set off down the mountain. It was a long way back to his valley, and there was no sign of his cows or his goats on the way. He became very anxious and ran as hard as he could. He found his once green valley dry and barren, his home shabby, and his wife aged and angry. It seemed he had been gone a long time, and she had not been able to make much of a living the while.

He told her of his adventure and showed her the flowers and the seed.

She was furious. "Why did you not take the gold and silver and precious stones?" she cried. "We would have been rich."

He could not explain to her that the flowers in the hand of the goddess had seemed more desirable to him at that moment than anything else on earth.

He bore her chiding patiently, put the flowers in a jug of water, and went outside to sow the seed. Although the measure was small he found he sowed field after field and the seeds never seemed to run out. The green shoots showed above ground quickly, and soon the meadows around were misted over with blue flowers.

One night in the moonlight he thought he saw the goddess with her handmaidens, but she was gone as soon as he reached out to her. When he woke next morning he knew what to do with the flowers in the meadows. They were flax flowers and he discovered how to prepare them for spinning and weaving and bleaching. He and his wife became prosperous, and he lived long and contentedly, working the flax and watching his children and his grandchildren and his great-grandchildren growing to maturity.

One day he noticed the bunch of flowers from the goddess was wilting and knew that his death was near. Slowly, laboriously, he climbed the mountain he had sprung up so easily in pursuit of the magical chamois. He found the arched entrance and passed through to the crystal hall of Holda. He was seen no more on earth.

Comment

It is important in dealing with myth and legend that we never become too rigid in our interpretation of certain symbols. In many stories "treasure of gold and silver and precious stones' represents a high spiritual achievement. Here it means the opposite. We get the impression that if the cow-herd had chosen the treasure he would have been the poorer in the end.

In many legends a deer or creature of some kind is the messenger of the gods, the guide who starts one off on the hunt for the true Self or the Deity. I am reminded of a story told by the San peoples of Southern Africa. A hunter while drinking at a water hole in the arid veldt sees the reflection of a beautiful white bird over his shoulder. He wants it and sets off in pursuit. The bird teases him by landing on thorn hushes and then flying off when he approaches. He forgets everything else and travels further and further away from his home, thinking of nothing but of catching the bird. Finally, as an old, old man, he follows it up the holy mountain of Kilimanjaro. With his last breath he reaches up as the bird rises from the summit into the infinite sky. He manages to catch a single feather that falls from it. He dies – content.

From the other side of the world the chamois with the horns that shine like the sun acts as messenger for the Earth Goddess. In Christian terms we talk of being "called". We have a "calling" or a "vocation". If the Deity called us direct it is possible most of us would be so alarmed and awed we would run away. Usually there is some intermediary, some person, some creature or incident, that leads us gently to the point where we realize what is happening. Our interest is aroused by something apparently irrelevant to the pursuit of spiritual enlightenment. We work. We concentrate. We learn. Just as we think we have mastered the knowledge we think we are pursuing, we realize there is more to learn. We go on. We forget the things that satisfied us in the past. We are obsessed now by attaining the unattainable. When we are nearly there, that which we thought was the object of our quest disappears, leaving us burning with curiosity for something we can't even define. We pass through the arch, the gate, between the mundane world and the spiritual and begin, at last, to understand why we have come this far.

Near as we can get to it we can never, in this life, have the whole transcendental truth we seek. The hunter is content with just one feather of the bird. The cow-herd is content with the bunch of flowers. The vision disappears as soon as he tries to touch the feet of the goddess. We have to be content with a small part of the truth we have been seeking with such single-minded persistence all our lives.

Most of the stories involving an animal messenger are about hunters and hunting. Those of us who hate blood sports are sometimes embarrassed by this. But the metaphor of hunting expresses very well the excitement, the urgency, the danger, and the loneliness of what we are about. Besides, the creature pursued by the hunter in these stories is always one step ahead of him and is never killed or caught.

The cow-herd and Holda story can be understood on various levels. The messenger leads the individual to spiritual enlightenment. He distinguishes between worldly wealth and the true riches of the spirit. The goddess is pleased and teaches him how to attain what he has glimpsed.

The story might also be quite simply a parable of how the Tyrol came to be such a successful flax-growing area. We are reminded of those organizations who have learned that it is unwise to hand over vast sums of money to underdeveloped countries without sending in experts to teach them how to build bridges and dams and how to use their land wisely and well for a prosperous and stable future.

Sources

Asgard of the Gods: Tales and Traditions of our Northern Ancestors, adapted from the work of Dr W. Wagner by M. W. Macdowall (Swan Sonnenschein, Le Bas & Lowrey, London, 1886).

The story of the hunter and the white bird is from *The Heart of the Hunter* by Laurens van der Post, 1968, p.167

Chapter 14

The Draught of Inspiration and the Crystal Cave

(Northern Europe)

A very wise being created by the gods was murdered by the dwarfs, who caught his blood in three bowls – one called Inspiration, one called Expiation, and the third called Offering. They mixed fermented honey with it and made it into mead. Any who drank of it received the gifts of song and eloquence.

In trouble with some giants one day, the dwarfs were forced to give up the mead to save their lives, and the precious liquid was kept in a crystal cave at the centre of a mountain, fiercely guarded by the giant's daughter, Gunlöd.

Odin, hearing of this from his two ravens who flew continually around the world to report on what was happening, desired to drink this magic mead. He disguised himself as a vagabond and descended to the region of the giants. There after many adventures he persuaded the uncle of Gunlöd to give him access to the drink in exchange for doing the work of nine men on his farm.

The year out, the giant's brother and Odin (still in disguise as a vagabond) climbed the mountain where the mead was kept. Gunlöd's uncle explained that it was impossible to penetrate the mountain, but Odin produced an auger and at last succeeded in making a tiny tunnel through the rock to the crystal cave. Odin then changed into a worm and wriggled through the tunnel. Once inside the magnificent halls of crystal, he took on his divine form and stood before Gunlöd wrapped in his mantle of stars. She bowed to him in awe.

He spent three days in the crystal cave and drank three draughts of the potent liquor. Then he rose up like an eagle and "flew with rhythmical motion to the divine heights, even as the skald (poet) raises himself to the dwellings of the immortals on the wings of song that is born of love, of wine, of inspiration" (M. W. Macdowall).

But the giant heard the flapping of his wings and suspected that he had been robbed of his mead. He flung an eagle-cape around his shoulders and pursued Odin through the air. Long and hard was the pursuit, but Odin managed to return safely to Asgard at last, where, to this day, goblets of the magic mead are kept. It is said that if mortal men or women are inspired to sing such songs as only gods and goddesses are wont to sing, it is the draught from these goblets that has given them the skill.

Comment

Note that the three bowls are called Inspiration, Expiation, and Offering. Note also that even Odin has to resort to hard work, ruse, and magic to obtain a sip from them.

True inspiration, the inspiration of the great poet, is not easily come by. It is a combination of three things: (1) expiation of all past sins so that one is pure and ready to receive; (2) grace – or a sudden inexplicable gift from above; (3) sacrifice of one's time, one's own personal comfort, etc.

When all these provisions have been met, there is nothing like the soaring excitement of the poet in full flight.

Note that the giant has to put on the *cloak* of an eagle to try to follow Odin, while Odin has *become* an eagle. The giant does not have the true inspiration. He has had the means to obtain it but chose to keep it hidden – unused. That it is in a crystal cave suggests that he knows it is something precious;

but that it is kept guarded and undrunk shows that he has not understood the purpose of it.

Gunlöd, who guards the mead, recognizes Odin and bows. She sees her role as protecting it from misuse by unworthy supplicants. She sees Odin as worthy.

The mead originated in the dark regions of the dwarfs (the subconscious), was kept hidden and imprisoned in the regions of the giants (the ordinary consciousness), and was only finally freed for the use of gods and mortals by Odin (the higher or supraconsciousness).

Source

Asgard of the Gods: Tales and Traditions of our Northern Ancestors, adapted from the work of Dr. W. Wagner by M. W. Macdowall (Swan Sonnenschein, Le Bas & Lowrey, London, 1886).

Chapter 15

The Fisherman and the Genie
and
The King of the Ebony Isles

(Middle East)

Two linked stories from the Arabian Nights series.

A poor fisherman used to cast his net four times each day. One day his catch was no more than a dead ass at the first cast, an old jar filled with mud at the second, broken bottles at the third, and a brass vessel with a lead stopper at the fourth.

About to despair at the catch, he noticed that the lead stopper of the brass vessel bore the seal of King Solomon. Intrigued, he prized it off with his knife and fell back in astonishment as smoke poured from the vessel, taking the form of a huge and monstrous genie. Mistaking the poor fisherman for Solomon, the Prophet of God, who had imprisoned him, the genie called out for mercy and vowed that he would never again cause him trouble. On being told that the man who had released him was a fisherman and not King Solomon, and that King Solomon had indeed been dead for more than two thousand years, the genie announced that his rescuer would have to die. It seems that over the centuries his bitterness had grown. He had been imprisoned in the first place because King Solomon had found he was the one demon he could not overcome. At first the genie had vowed to reward his rescuer with "all the treasures attainable in heaven and earth", but when no one came he reduced the reward to earthly treasures only. After more centuries had passed, his promise was for three wishes only. Now after more than twenty centuries he was so angry he had vowed to kill the first man he saw.

The fisherman thought fast and then asked that he might have the answer to one question before he met his death, and charged him on God's name, "which is the seal of Solomon", to answer truthfully. The genie agreed, and the fisherman wanted to know how such a huge being could fit into such a tiny vessel. Not content with a verbal answer, he persisted in misunderstanding, until the genie in exasperation proved the point by flowing back as smoke into the vessel. As soon as he was in, the fisherman slapped on the lead stopper and imprisoned him again.

Enraged, the genie struggled for release but was held fast by the seal of Solomon. He began to plead and cajole and promised at last that he would give the fisherman all the treasure he could desire if he would only set him free. So desperate and sad did he sound that the kindly fisherman agreed to release him, but only after he took a solemn vow that he would not harm him.

The genie, free once more, commanded the fisherman to follow him, saying he would make his fortune.

They left the village and all that the fisherman had known behind and climbed a mountain.

At the top of the mountain they found a desert plain surrounded by four hills. At the centre of the desert plain they found a lake. The genie told the fisherman to cast his nets. When he had done so he found that he had caught four beautiful and unusual fishes. One was as white as diamond, one as red as ruby, one as yellow as citron, and one as blue as sapphire.

The genie suggested that the fisherman should offer the fish to the Sultan, and then the earth opened and swallowed him up.

The fisherman presented the four fishes to the Sultan who, delighted, paid him four hundred gold pieces and commanded his cook to grill them for his dinner. The fisherman departed for home, well pleased with the fortunate outcome of his adventure.

He had not gone far, however, when a servant of the Sultan caught up with him and asked him to return and catch four more such fish because the first four had been burned to cinders.

"How come?" the fisherman asked.

"It was very strange," he was told. "No sooner were the fish on the grill than a beautiful young woman burst through the kitchen wall and called out to them. The fish themselves replied that the bond still held and that "with give and take the reckoning would be met". Then she flung the fish into the fire and they were consumed by the flames."

The fisherman returned to the lake and caught four more and was again rewarded with four hundred gold pieces.

But these four fishes met the same fate.

The only difference the third time the fisherman presented four such fishes was that it was not a young woman who spoke to the fishes, but a large black man.

The vizier, who had witnessed these three extraordinary events, at last plucked up courage to tell the Sultan. So intrigued was he that he insisted the fisherman show him exactly where he had caught the fish.

The Sultan and his entourage set off with the fisherman, who insisted that the lake was but a few hours' journey from the court, though the others swore they had climbed those mountains many times and seen no lake.

To everyone's surprise, they found the desert plain, the four hills, and the mysterious lake. Tents were set up and the Sultan's party came up.

In the dead of night the Sultan crept away, determined to explore the strange and unknown country by himself.

After a journey of three days he came upon a gleaming palace of white crystalline marble. He entered through the gates, where no one challenged him, and set off in search of someone who would announce him to the king of this magnificent place.

But he found no one. He wandered through deserted halls where pearls and not water flowed from the fountains. Chests of shimmering precious stones lay open and abandoned. Crystal candlesticks held no candles.

At last he thought he heard the distant sound of a voice raised in lamentation, and strode through the deserted corridors until he found a handsome youth seated on a couch. The youth greeted him dolefully without rising. While apologizing for this lack of courtesy the young man lifted his robe and showed the Sultan that from the waist downwards he was pure white crystalline marble, while above the waist he was flesh and blood.

Solicitously the Sultan enquired how such a fate could have befallen the elegant youth and was told the story.

It seemed the youth, the king of the Ebony Isles, had married his cousin, a beautiful young maiden who for five years had delighted him in every way. Then he discovered that she was drugging his wine every night and creeping out of the palace.

One night he followed her and found that she was visiting a lover outside the gates of the city, a huge black slave. Enraged he leapt into the room and struck the slave a blow with his sword which he believed had killed him, but he fled before the queen was aware of who her lover's assailant was.

He returned to the palace and said nothing about the event. He noticed she was very pale and distraught in the morning, and on his enquiry she told him that her father and mother and two of her brothers had been suddenly killed. She begged his leave to retreat to a House of Lamentation. Tight-lipped he agreed, hoping that she would soon forget the slave.

But two years went by and she did not return to his bed.

One day the young king could bear it no more and secretly entered her house to see what was going on. There he found the slave barely alive but being tenderly nursed by the queen. His vocal chords had been severed by the sword blow. It was clear that the queen's interest in the man was as passionate as ever.

The king revealed himself and began to berate her for her behaviour. Instead of being shamed by his words she flew into an extraordinary rage, realizing for the first time that it was her husband who had reduced her lover to the state of half-life he was now in. She cursed him so violently that the half of his body below the waist turned to marble, the city surrounding the palace became a lake, the Ebony Isles became the four hill surrounding it, and all his subjects became fishes, the Muslims white, the Persian fire-worshippers red, the Jews yellow, and the Christians blue.

"Not content with this," the youth told the Sultan, "every day she leaves the side of her lover for a while and comes to my chamber to thrash me with a whip until I bleed."

The Sultan, moved by the youth's story, promised to help him.

The next time the woman was thrashing the king, the Sultan made his way into the House of Lamentation and slew the woman's lover. He then threw the body in a deep well and took his place under the coverlets. When she returned, the Sultan spoke in a muffled voice as though he was the slave who had just recovered the use of his vocal chords. Her joy at this was short-lived because he at once began to abuse her, saying that he had suffered these two years because of her unremitting violence against her husband, his cries had kept him awake at night, and heaven had afflicted him because of her sins. Horrified, she asked how she could make amends and was told that she had to undo the spell on her husband at once if she wanted her lover ever to walk again.

She hurried away to do so, and then the Sultan said she must take the spell off her husband's kingdom as well if she wanted her lover hale and hearty again.

Again she hurried to obey him and returned as swiftly as she could, looking forward to making love at last to a healthy man. But the Sultan waited until she was leaning over him and thrust his sword into her until she was dead.

He then arose and returned to the young king. He found him standing among his treasures rejoicing. The teeming city was going about its business, the hills had become ebony-forested islands. All was thriving and fertile.

The Sultan invited the young king back to his own country to become his son and heir and, after a long journey, much longer than it had taken to reach the marble palace and the lake of coloured fishes, they arrived back at the Sultan's domain, the king of the Ebony Isles cured of his malady, the fisherman rewarded, and the Sultan no longer a lonely, childless ruler.

Comment

The strongest thread in the second story is connected with sexual satisfaction – in particular female sexual satisfaction. The beautiful young prince does not satisfy his wife, who therefore seeks satisfaction elsewhere. Note that she goes out at night, secretly in the dark, to a black slave, rejecting the handsome young man with all the riches. Her natural sexuality has been denied. She has to seek it secretly, shamefully, in the dark from someone totally outside the rules of her wealthy and effete society. Her lover is outside the city gate.

In his jealousy the king attempts to kill the slave, hut only succeeds in severing his vocal chords so that he cannot speak. Do we have here a comment on the kind of society where it is taboo to speak about sexual matters and, consequently, the society is wasting away?

The queen builds a private sanctuary for her lover and tries to nurse him back to health. Again, note the secrecy. It is inconceivable to her that she could speak to her husband about her needs.

For the second time the king finds her with her lover and upbraids her, thereby revealing that he is responsible for the condition the lover is now in. Note that when he married her she was a pleasant young woman. Now she is a frustrated and vicious enchanter because of his failure to recognize her needs. In her rage she casts a spell on him. It is significant that it is his lower half, his sexual organs, that are turned to marble. Because he doesn't understand her sexuality, his own becomes useless. He can only enjoy his if she can enjoy hers. He lives among great riches, fountains of pearls, caskets of precious stones, but they give them no joy and have no value for him. Though his mind is unimpaired, his life is a burden to him because the passionate, feeling part of himself – the power and energy of the sexual drive – is turned to stone.

That the four great religions have been turned into four different-coloured fish by the woman in her mood of bitter vengeance might indicate that the four religions have also been rendered impotent by frustrated and misdirected sexual energy.

"The Fisherman and the Genie" and "The Story of the King of the Ebony Isles' are two stories in the *Arabian Nights* series that are very closely linked. It is worth noting the careful counterpointing of the elements in each.

The genie the fisherman finds in the brazen vessel with the lead stopper has been sealed in by King Solomon thousands of years before. King Solomon was a great Adept and a wise sage, who fought and overcame many "demons". The one he could not overcome he imprisoned in the bottle. As the two linked stories unfold we begin to understand that the demon Solomon could not control was his own forceful and dangerous sexual energy.

The fisherman casts his net four times and it is only on the fourth casting that he catches the genie. Similarly there are four religions mentioned. The white fish are the Muslims, the red the Persian fire-worshippers (followers of Zoroaster), the yellow the Jews and the blue the Christians. The fisherman catches them but does not understand what they really are. He takes them to the Sultan (who echoes Solomon in this story). The Sultan tries to eat them, that is, take them into his life, but fails. The fishes are not to be bought.

The bond holds yet;
Paid by thee, we pay the debt.
With give and take is the reckoning met.

The Sultan has to set off on an inner journey and face many trials before he can undo the harm that has been done. It is the give and take in the sexual relationship, and indeed in the whole of life, that must be recognized. The woman herself is persuaded to free her husband and the land from the spell when she realizes for the first time how interdependent everything is. Her lover cannot get better if her husband does not get better. In other words her obsession with her own sexual satisfaction is as destructive as her husband's was with his own. That the Sultan kills the queen rather than restoring her to a fuller and more balanced life with her husband is disappointing. Perhaps it is that Scheherazade has gone as far as she dares in indicating the strength of women's sexuality, and, because she is telling the story to her lord and master, she has to punish the woman in the end.

We may note another counterpoint between the two stories. The genie in his long imprisonment changes the reward he intends to give to whoever releases him from "all the treasures attainable in heaven and earth", to "earthly riches only", to "the fulfilment of three wishes", and finally to the curse of hideous suffering and death. If the connection is made with the imprisonment and frustration of the healthy sexual urge we see the increasing harm done as the frustration continues. Both the queen and the genie become dangerous and evil forces the longer the frustration continues. The treasures we should have from a healthy and beautiful sexual relationship are lost, and only suffering is the result.

The four catches of dead ass, jar of mud, broken bottles, and unpredictable demonic genie, may well be a heavily disguised and bitter comment on the four religions that had become of no more value than detritus since King Solomon's time and needed a journey of the soul and a challenging spiritual adventure to transform them back to their original living state.

If this were a Christian story, we would note the significance that it is a fisherman that starts the whole process of revival. Christ, the fisher of souls. As it is not, we can still remember that the sea is universally the symbol for the great ocean of consciousness in which the soul swims, emerging from the depths of other realities beyond our normal awareness.

The fisherman's catch is detritus – in each case something that was once useful, but now is useless and valueless. The genie, on the other hand, was once thought to be evil and destructive but is now after its long sojourn in the sea (which is more than the sea) about to bring about transformation in the lives of the fisherman, the Sultan, and the young crystalline king.

As in all myths and legends, every detail has significance, and it takes a long time to tease out all the meanings. Just as I was about to leave this story I noticed that the fishes on the grill are struck by a rod of myrtle. Why myrtle? I looked up in *An Illustrated Encyclopaedia of Traditional Symbols* by J. C. Cooper and found out that "myrtle is a vital essence and transmits the breath of life, and is symbolic of life germinating and rebirth and life renewed". It also symbolizes "the feminine principle". To the Egyptians it is sacred to Hathor, the goddess of love and fertility. To the Hebrews it symbolizes "marriage". On all counts these interpretations are appropriate to this story.

Sources

The Arabian Nights, retold by Laurence Housman (Hodder & Stoughton, 1907; republished in the Classic Collectors Series by Omega Books, 1985).

J.C. Cooper, *An Illustrated Encyclopaedia of Traditional Symbols* (Thames & Hudson, 1978).

Chapter 16

Lucifer's Emerald

(Middle East)

There was once an archangel called Lucifer, Light Bringer, Star of the Morning. He walked in the City of Heaven as a prince, a favourite of the King of Kings, God of Gods. He was the fairest of the archangels, his raiment fine and rich, the diadem around his forehead studded with precious gems. In the centre was an emerald of the same substance as the emerald rainbow that spanned the sky above the throne of the King of Kings and reflected in the sea of crystal beneath the throne.

It was through this emerald, as through a window in the mind, that Lucifer saw the full glory of God, and we, many regions and realms below the Heavenly City, catching the faint glimmer of it, were, in those days encouraged to seek such a glory.

The City of Heaven is beyond our imagining, but it has been said that it is built of gold as transparent as crystal, that its walls are of fine jasper, that it has twelve foundations, each of a different precious stone. From the first to the last they are as follows: jasper, sapphire, chalcedony, emerald, sardonyx, sardius, chrysolyte, beryl, topaz, chrysoprase, jacinth, and amethyst. The city's twelve gates are each of a separate pearl from the Ocean of Consciousness that has been since before the Word was first spoken.

Beside a river as clear as crystal, flowing with the Waters of Life from the throne of the Most High, the Tree of Life grows, bearing twelve different fruits for the healing of all the realms of Heaven and Hell.

In this city are many different orders of being, among them nine different orders of angels, the highest being the Seraphim who draw the hearts of mortals towards the Divine Love, the Kerubim, who pour forth wisdom, and the highest order of all, nameless ones, all-seeing, who occupy thrones close to the Throne of the Most High, Mary herself being one of these.

Below these are other orders of angels, each created for a specific purpose, each with a fixed role to play and a fixed relationship with the Most High.

All were satisfied with this rigid hierarchy, until the Lord of All Himself decided to introduce an interesting maverick into the situation. He created Man in his own image, different from the angels, independent, free.

Pleased with his new creation and knowing that the very freedom he had given Man enabled him, potentially, to rise as high as the greatest angels – though at the same time it was possible for him to sink lower than the lowest – God demanded that the angels should bow down before Man. Some say it was Lucifer led the rebellion of those who, from jealousy of the freedom Man had, refused to bow down to him. Some say it was not, but, in the confusion and the fighting that followed among them the loyal angels and the disloyal ones, many fell from the Heavenly City to earth and there made mischief among men, determined that they, the new created would never, no matter how hard they tried, aspire to Heaven to sit on the angelic thrones. In the Fall damage was done to Lucifer's diadem, and the Great Emerald was loosened and fell like a green meteor in a shower of light to earth.

Ever since that time Man has sought it, for with its recovery it is believed will come the power to see the Glory of God, and, by seeing, to reach towards it beyond the influence of the fallen angels.

Comment

A legend is often like a kind of cosmic rumour.

There is an image, or an idea, mentioned either in the ancient oral tradition or in work of literature, and because it resonates so appropriately with our experience and expresses so felicitously something of importance to us that we have found frustratingly difficult to express, it takes hold and grows generation by generation into something of greater potency than it originally appeared to be, yet never far from what it potentially was. Other elements accrete to it, giving and taking power to and from the central stem.

Such an image, an idea, is the war in heaven and Lucifer's lost emerald.

It appears first, to my knowledge, in the Bible, in the Old Testament:

> *How art thou fallen from heaven, O Lucifer, son of the morning!... For thou hast said in thine heart, I will ascend into heaven. I will exalt my throne above the stars of God... I will be like the most High. (Isaiah 14:12–14)*

And then in the New Testament:

> *For if God spared not the angels that sinned... (2 Peter 2:4)*

> *And the angels that kept not their first estate, but left their own habitation... (Jude 6)*

It appears in the Middle Ages. Lucifer's crown had been given to him by 60,000 angels. One stone fell to earth, and from it was carved a vessel of great beauty which came after many ages into the hands of Joseph of Arimathea. He offered it to the Saviour, who made use of it in the Last Supper. Later it became known as the Holy Grail.

In *c*.1200 Wolfram von Eschenbach claimed that his story *Parzival* came from a Provençal singer named Kyot, who in turn had it from an Arab poet in Toldeo named Flegitanis. It describes the Grail as a miraculous stone that fell from heaven, the "lapsit exillis":

> *Those who took neither side when Lucifer and the Trinity fought – these angels, noble and worthy, were compelled to descend to earth, to this same stone... Since then the stone has always been in the care of those God called to*

*this task and to whom He sent His angel. Sir, such is the
nature of the Grail.*

By the power of the stone called "lapsit exillis'

*the phoenix burns to ashes, but the ashes give him life
again...There never was a human so ill but that if he one
day sees that stone, he cannot die within the week that
follows. And in looks he will not fade. His appearance will
stay the same as when the best years of his life began, and
though he should see the stone for two hundred years, it
will never change, save that his hair might perhaps turn
grey. Such power does the stone give a man that flesh and
bones are at once made young again. (*Parzival, *Book IX,
pp. 251–3)*

In Milton's *Paradise Lost* the war in Heaven is described in
great detail:

*He it was whose pride
Had cast him out from heav'n, with all his host
Of rebel Angels, by whose aid aspiring
To set himself in glory above his peers,
He trusted to have equalled the Most High,
If he opposed; and with ambitious aim
Against the throne and monarchy of God
Raised impious war in heav'n, and battle proud,
With vain attempt. Him the almighty Power
Hurled headlong flaming from th" ethereal sky,
With hideous ruin and combustion, down
To bottomless perdition, there to dwell
In adamantine chains and penal fire,
Who durst defy th' Omnipotent to arms.*

(Book 1, lines 36 – 49)

*his hand was known
In heav'n by many a towered structure high,
Where sceptred angels held their residence,
And sat as princes, whom the supreme King*

> *Exalted to such power, and gave to rule*
> *Each in his hierarchy, the orders bright.*
> *Nor was his name unheard or unadored*
> *In ancient Greece; and in Ausonian land*
> *Men called him Mulciber; and how he fell*
> *From heav'n they fabled, thrown by angry Jove*
> *Sheer o'er the crystal battlements; from morn*
> *To noon he fell, from noon to dewy eve,*
> *A summer's day; and with the setting sun*
> *Dropt from the zenith like a falling star*
>
> (Book I lines 732-45)

The references to the story are so numerous that I cannot quote them all, but I will give one more, this time from *The Secret Teachings of All Ages* by Manly P. Hall (p. xcix) because he has gone into the ancient mystery teachings more than most:

> *The Lapis Exilis, crown jewel of the Archangel Lucifer, fell from heaven. Michael, archangel of the sun and the Hidden God of Israel, at the head of the angelic hosts swooped down upon Lucifer and his legions of rebellious spirits. During the conflict, Michael with his flaming sword struck the flashing Lapis Exilis from the coronet of his adversary, and the green stone fell through all the celestial rings into the dark and immeasurable Abyss. Out of Lucifer's radiant gem was fashioned the Sangreal, or Holy Grail, from which Christ is said to have drunk at the Last Supper.*

The Grail group of legends is one of the most powerful in the Western tradition and draws for its strength, as all good myths do, on our deepest human experiences and for its symbols on our earliest cultural memories.

The Quest is our most universal and enduring human experience. The quest for meaning and purpose in our lives; the quest for reassurance that there is some kind of permanence or afterlife; the quest for love and satisfaction, both physical and spiritual; the quest for knowledge and wisdom and maturity.

We symbolize it in our myths and legends constantly, often linking it with that haunting feeling that we have once had the very wisdom and knowledge and sense of purpose we seek, but that somehow we have lost it... Shambhala... Shangri-la... Eden... Atlantis.

The Grail legends rise from this need to seek for something higher and better in our lives, and for the symbolism in them we draw on cultural memories from both pagan and Christian sources.

It is almost impossible to say what the Grail is other than that it is what we seek and the finding of it will transform us into a higher state of being. Paradoxically, however, we have no chance of finding it unless we are already in a higher state of being.

In the Middle Ages a series of stories seemed to bubble to the surface of our Western consciousness around a single theme, the search for the mysterious Grail, and they were written down from the rich and ancient oral tradition in Wales, in France, in Germany, evolving and changing but always linked to the same characters and the same quest.

In Britain they first appeared among the stories we now call the *Mabinogion*. Peredur, the son of Evrawc, becomes Parzival in the great work of Wolfram von Eschenbach in early thirteenth century Germany, Percival in *The Story of the Grail* by Chrétien de Troyes in France, Percival in Sir Thomas Malory's *Le Morte d'Arthur*. Most of them suggest that the Grail is the chalice that Christ used at the Last Supper; some, Wolfram in particular, that it was a stone fallen from heaven, Lucifer's lost emerald. Some combine the two ideas. The chalice Christ used to institute the first Eucharist was carved out of the Sacred Emerald that fell from heaven.

My theory is that Lucifer's mysterious and powerful emerald glimmers in the mythic imagination throughout history and throughout the world, appearing in ancient Egypt in the possession of Horus ('Horus, Lord of the Green Stone": *Pyramid Texts*, Utterance 301), and as the Wisdom Book of the God Djehuti (Thoth) that glowed in the dark, was lost and sought as fervently as any Grail, and reappeared at last in the form of an inferior copy about 300 BC as the Emerald Tablet of Hermes Trismegistus – the tablet on which was inscribed in raised letters the tenets of the philosophy that became so influential as Hermeticism.

There is mention of an emerald tablet originally inscribed by Cham, one of the sons of Noah. And there is a link with Melchizadek, king of Salem, who instructed Abraham in esoteric lore, and in whose order Jesus was said to be a high priest. It appears in the legends of Chartres Cathedral, brought by the nine Templars who lived for nine years on the ruined site of Solomon's Temple in Jerusalem imbibing the arcane knowledge of Solomon and Sheba. The name Chartres itself comes from words indicating "guardians of the stone", and Frédéric Lionel, the eminent French esotericist, in his *Legends and Symbols of the Cathedral of Chartres* (Golden Way Foundation), claims that the magnificent statue of Melchizadek in the central bay of the north porch, is holding an emerald – *the* emerald!

Another intriguing echo comes from Cairo in the ninth century. Caliph al Mamoun, son of the man to whom Scheherezade told her thousand and one stories, made the first incursion into the Great Pyramid in search of a gigantic emerald that was supposed to be buried at the centre. It is through his tunnel that we now enter the pyramid as tourists.

Another branch of the story takes us to India with Alexander the Great who used the power of the emerald to conquer the whole world – but was ultimately lost because he had not learned to conquer himself.

Lucifer's lost emerald presages the loss of Eden by Adam and Eve. It has to be symbolic of the most important quest through all the realms. In the search, we find ourselves. In the finding, we find God.

Sources

The Bible: Isaiah 14: 12 and the Book of Revelation.

John Milton, *Paradise Lost*, Book I.

Wolfram von Eschenbach, *Parzival: A Romance of the Middle Ages*, translated by H. M. Mustard and C. E. Passage (Vintage Books, New York, 1961), Book IX, pp. 251–3.

——, *Parzival* translated by A. T. Hatto (Penguin Books, 1980).

Peter Lamborn Wilson, *Angels* (Thames & Hudson, 1980).

Gustav Davidson, *A Dictionary of Angels* (The Free Press, New York, 1967).

Emma Jung and Marie-Louise Von Franz, *The Grail Legend* (Hodder & Stoughton, 1971).

Caitlin and John Matthews, *The Western Way* (Arkana, 1986).

Manly P. Hall, *The Secret Teachings of All Ages* (1901; The Philosophical Research Society Inc., Los Angeles, 1977), p. xcix.

John Matthews, *The Grail: Quest for the Eternal* (Thames & Hudson, 1981).

——, *At the Table of the Grail* (Routledge, 1984).

T. W. Rolleston, *Myths and Legends of the Celtic Race* (Harrap & Co., 1911), p. 407.

Frédéric Lionel, *Legends and Symbols of the Cathedral of Chartres* (Golden Way Foundation).

S. A. B. Mercer, *Pyramid Texts* Vol. 1 (Longmans, 1952), utterance 301, paragraph 457c.

Chapter 17

The Book of Thoth

(Middle East: Ancient Egypt)

Khaemwaset, First Prophet of Ptah, High Priest of Ra, Chief of Seers, and honoured son of Pharaoh Rameses II, was a scholar and an archaeologist, passionately interested in the ancient and esoteric wisdom of his ancestors and working hard to preserve and reinstate it. He had read in ancient texts about the Book of Thoth, the Book of the God of Wisdom, Djehuti, and he wanted more than anything in the world to have access to it.

One day he was told by an old magician that he believed it to be buried in the tomb of a prince called Ne-nefer-ka-Ptah. The old man's researches had revealed to him that the possession of the book would give two great advantages. One would be the complete knowledge of all the natural world, and the other would be the knowledge of the realms that are normally invisible to man, the supernatural realms – and the secret names of things in the mind of the creator.

The old sage told Khaemwaset that he had found the clues to where the book was hidden too late to make use of them himself, but he knew that if anyone could find the book it would be Khaemwaset, and if anyone could be trusted with the book it would be Khaemwaset.

Daring the fearsome protective spells that always accompany Egyptian burials, Prince Khaemwaset searched for the tomb and secretly entered it. Helping and accompanying him was his brother.

They undid the necropolis seals in the dead of night, rolled the heavy doorstones aside, slithered down a ramp, negotiated a black pit, and finally, after long, dark and stuffy corridors, reached the tomb chamber itself. In all this they were silently watched by the figures of the gods, carved and painted on every possible wall surface, their living presence in the artist's images of them ensured by magic spells. Khaemwaset needed all his training to unlock each invisible door, neutralize each curse, placate each god.

To their surprise and Khaemwaset's joy they found the tomb chamber that should have been pitch dark so deep underground, illuminated by the glow from the very book they had come to find.

In the tomb lay the embalmed body of the Prince Ne-nefer-ka-Ptah, a sage and magician in his own right when he was alive. His was the only body present, but Khaemwaset and his brother found the tomb chamber occupied by three ghosts, that of the occupant himself and of his wife and son.

Khaemwaset announced that he had come to take the book away and reached out for it. At once the ghost-prince held up his hand and the ghost-wife protested. It seemed the bodies of the prince's wife and child had been lost and had never had proper burial. He was holding their souls close to him through eternity by the power invested in the book.

Khaemwaset had struggled too long to find the sacred book and wanted it too much to be so easily deterred. He told the dead prince he had to have the book and would do anything, risk anything, to obtain it. When the ghost-prince refused to part with it once more, Khaemwaset tried to take it by force, but found himself flung back by invisible and supernatural hands.

And then the dead prince began to tell his own story in an endeavour to discourage the living prince from making the same mistake he himself had made.

It seemed that Ne-nefer-ka-Ptah, like Khaemwaset a magician-priest greedy for supernatural knowledge, had learned from a dying sage that the mysterious Book of Thoth was lying hidden in the Sea of Coptos, a journey of three days and three nights from where he was. He was warned that it was for a very good reason that it was so hidden and protected, but Ne-nefer-ka-Ptah would not listen.

He made the journey with his wife and child, and after many vicissitudes found it on an isolated island in the middle of the Sea of Coptos. It was securely guarded by vipers, serpents, and scorpions, and every dangerous creature. He managed to fight his way through somehow until he almost reached the box in which he believed it was contained. But there was still one impediment. Around the box there was an endless snake. He killed the snake with his dagger, but it sprang alive again as he reached for the box. Once again he smote it, and once again it appeared to die but did not.

The third time he cut it in half and buried each half separately in sand. Before the one half of the immortal snake could find the other half, he seized the box and made off with it.

He found that the box was in fact a nest of boxes, seven in all – iron, bronze, kete-wood, ivory and ebony, silver, and gold. Each was locked with a spell he had to overcome before he could reach the centre and the precious object itself.

He now had the book in his possession and made off with it. But no sooner had he done so than all kinds of misfortunes began to befall him, including the death of his wife and child and the disappearance of their bodies in the Sea of Coptos.

Finally, unable to understand what the book taught, and terrified of the consequences of stealing it, he killed himself. He was buried in this tomb. The book was buried with him among his possessions, no one else realizing what it was. His "ka" discovered that by using the spells in the book he could draw the souls of his wife and child to be with him, but apart from that he had not been able to master its secrets. He told Khaemwaset that he would be ill advised to take it from the tomb. Nothing but harm would come to him from it.

Khaemwaset refused to take his advice and demanded the book once more. Once more he was refused.

At last he persuaded the ghost to play chess with him for it and the ghost agreed – convinced that he would win.

They played one game and the ghost of Ne-nefer-ka-Ptah won. As he did so Khaemwaset's feet sank into the stone floor. They played another game and again Ne-nefer-ka-Ptah won.

This time Khaemwaset sank into the floor up to his middle. By the end of the third game only Khaemwaset's head was free of the stone.

At this point he whispered to his brother to go and fetch his amulets and his sacred books from the Temple of Ptah. Terrified at the turn things had taken, the brother ran as fast as he could and returned at last with Khaemwaset's set of crystal amulets and his book of spells. As soon as the crystals were upon him he began to rise from the floor, and as soon as he was free enough he pronounced the most powerful spells he knew.

The book was freed from the supernatural hold of Ne-nefer-ka-Ptah, and the two priests rushed from the tomb, Khaemwaset clutching his precious burden to his chest.

How much Khaemwaset, son of Rameses II, learned from the Book of Thoth is not known, but no sooner had he it in his possession than he found disasters befalling him, as Ne-nefer-ka-Ptah had predicted.

At last, after a particularly horrifying night in which he believed he had killed his own children at the behest of a woman he desired, he went back to the tomb and returned the book to the ghost of Ne-nefer-ka-Ptah.

"It is well that it is hidden," he said. "We learn more by seeking it than by possessing it."

In recompense for what he had done he located the bodies of Ne-nefer-ka-Ptah's wife and child and buried them beside the prince in his tomb.

Comment

To my mind the Book of Thoth Khaemwaset sought and found might well be part of the long and intriguing story of Lucifer's lost emerald. The book glows like a jewel, and a thousand years later, when an Egyptian wisdom book is found ascribed to Hermes Trismegistus, it is called the "Emerald Tablet". It became the primary text for the Hermeticists, a school of esoteric teaching that flourished in medieval, Renaissance, and still, in modern times. I wonder if it was not indeed the ancient Book of Thoth that Khaemwaset sought – or at least a copy of it. For Hermes is the later Greek name for the Egyptian god Djehuti (Thoth), and an emerald is an appropriate symbol for a wisdom that can shine in the tomb and illuminate even the darkest mystery of all, death.

But whether the original Book of Thoth was inscribed on an emerald or not, this story still belongs among the crystal legends because of the amulets of crystal that helped Khaemwaset escape from the constricting magic of the ghost.

Every aspect of life in ancient Egypt was dependent on magic, and amulets of different types of crystal were carried by everyone.

Fish images saved one from drowning. Leg images were offered to the gods of healing if one had a crippled leg. God and goddess amulets ensured the protection and attention of one's favourite god. In death the body was protected by numerous amulets, each with a specific magical purpose to perform. Sadly it was the very presence of these objects carved out of valuable gems that caused robbers to violate the tombs and tear the bandages irreverently off the mummies. I like to think that perhaps they had already done their work and the souls of the deceased were safely in the Duat, or reborn, before the robbers came.

It is worth noting that Khaemwaset, who was a high priest and a master of magic, was not able to escape imprisonment unaided. He had to send for his amulets and book of spells. Perhaps it was because he had allowed himself, by his own free will, to accept the game of chess and its stakes. Many legends from many different countries warn us against gambling with strangers! He had given up control of himself because of his overwhelming desire for the book, and was no longer reaching to the high spiritual realms but sinking deeper and deeper into the physical world, into "worldliness", as he lost at each test and trial.

He believed the amulets and spells would help him, and his brother fetched them for him.

There is an ancient coffin text that says: "Precious stones come for you, they float on the wave for you from the interior of the mountains, making themselves the protectors of the thickets of papyrus, at the leaves of the first door of the necropolis' (Coffin Texts Spell 840, quoted by C. Jacq in his book *Egyptian Magic*, p. 57).

The Eye of Horus is perhaps one of the most powerful of amulets. It grants the wearer the skill to see with the eyes of a god. The heart represents the will in ancient Egypt, and a heart of green felspar ensures that a person's heart will not be taken away in the Underworld. When a heron is carved on the back of a heart amulet or heart scarab of red carnelian, the wearer's ka is granted free passage to come and go as it wishes between the worlds. A frog gives the power of rebirth and resurrection. A fly gives swift action. A papyrus plant of green felspar gives durability and security: "I am the column of green felspar, which cannot be crushed, and which is raised by the hand of Djehuti... If it is safe, I am safe..." (W. M.Flinders Petrie, *Amulets*).

It is not only the type of crystal that has magical significance in ancient Egypt; the image itself is thought to carry the life force of that which is depicted. The many gods of Egypt, like the many saints and angels of the Catholics, and the Boddhisattvas of the Buddhists, wish to help us, but can only do so if somehow we make a passage for them from their realm to our own. This passage could be made by prayer alone, but not many people are capable of achieving unaided the pure quality of prayer that is necessary to open this channel: more often than not we need some relic, some image, some symbol or reminder, to stimulate the right frame of mind (or heart).

Khaemwaset had lost his own spiritual inner strength by desiring something so badly he was careless enough to fall into a trap. He needed help. He needed his crystal amulets – the Horus Eye of black tourmaline, white quartz, and blue lapis lazuli. He needed the heart and papyrus column of green felspar, the golden topaz fly, the heron on the heart of red carnelian, the crayfish claw of red jasper that protects against the evil eye.

The Book of Thoth – a kind of ancient Egyptian Holy Grail

or Ark of the Covenant that destroys the unauthorized who touch it but gives great rewards to those for whom it is meant – has been the subject of much speculation. Some suggest that the Tarot pack is all that is left to us of it – picture cards containing images that hold the Mysteries in secret hibernation, like a cave holds a bear in winter. Come the spring of our enlightenment, the bear wakes, the images wake, and we know "the essence and power of all things' (Psellus, a Byzantine philosopher quoted on p. 19 of Frédéric Lionel's book *The Magic Tarot*).

Some link it to the "Emerald Tablet" of the alchemists, containing instructions for transforming one thing into another on the grounds that, differing only in scale, all things, from the Cosmos to the atom, are governed by the same intrinsic laws.

Both Ne-nefer-ka-Ptah and Khaemwaset are informed by old and dying men where the book may be found – but warned about the dangers of trying to acquire it. It is as though it is not intended that the secret whereabouts of the book should be totally lost, yet knowledge of its hiding place should be kept by a line of initiates throughout the centuries, only to be revealed on death to the next in line.

Almost all cultures have a myth in which some knowledge is felt to be so powerful, so dangerous if held by the wrong person, that it must be kept secret and only released after the most stringent and rigorous of testing to the care of the chosen guardian. This concept might have sprung from our own bewilderment faced by the extraordinary mystery of existence. We know we are here, but we don't know why, or how we came to be in the first place. We don't know if there is someone in control who has a purpose and a design for us – or if our lives are pointless, rudderless, and random. We can believe – but we cannot know for sure. Because we fear that knowing everything may well spoil the adventure of living and remove all incentive to explore and progress, and yet we fear that if there is never any chance of knowing we will despair equally and give up trying, we like to posit that the knowledge is accessible only to a select and superior few, who will guard it and keep it safely "in trust" for us. But even this has its dangers –

even honoured and dependable people can prove to be as fallible as ourselves. There is the danger that the knowledge we desire and yet fear might be misused and somehow we, or the world we know, might be destroyed. I think that is why there are so many myths like the above, stressing the danger of the Secret and the need for careful and honourable guardianship.

The great snake that guards the book on the island in the middle of the Sea of Coptos reminds us of the great and monstrous snake called Apep in ancient Egyptian theology – the snake that represents chaos and non-existence. It fights Ra every night in the dark Underworld. Its victory would mean the sun would not rise in the morning and all existence would cease to be. So far it has been defeated in every encounter. But it is never destroyed and is always waiting to engulf us. Our existence can never be taken for granted.

Cunningly Ne-nefer-ka-Ptah manages to win a little time for himself by burying the two parts of the severed snake under the sand so they take longer to reunite. The book is almost his. He still has to undergo seven stages of initiation – the seven boxes.

But the book is stolen. It has not been given to him by the gods. Its wisdom is still inaccessible to him and hinders rather than helps him. In despair and frustration he kills himself and becomes the guardian of the book.

Khaemwaset pits his wits against him in the games of chess (or Senet) as Ne-nefer-ka-Ptah pitted his wits against the immortal snake. Khaemwaset loses and brings in reinforcements of magical amulets. The use of magic wins him the book – but cannot give him mastery of its contents. More harm than good comes to him as a result of possessing it. Something more than intellectual cunning and magic spells is needed if one is to truly understand the contents of the Sacred Book of Thoth.

Fulcanelli, in his extraordinary book about Alchemical symbols used in medieval cathedrals (*Le Mystére des Cathédrales*), said the alchemists' Great Book of Nature is easy to read providing one knows where to find it and how to open it – both extremely difficult tasks. It "holds the revelation of the profane sciences and of the sacred mysteries". The great work of the alchemists is often symbolically expressed as a book sealed with seven hands. Seven successive operations are needed to open it – each breaking the seal of one of the bands. We are reminded of the Book of Thoth contained in seven boxes.

Sources

C. Jacq, *Egyptian Magic*, translated by Janet M. Davis (Aris & Philips, 1985).

Griffith, *Stories of the High Priests of Memphis* (The Clarendon Press, Oxford).

Article in *New Dimensions* by F. P. D. (1980?).

Roger Lancelyn Green, *Tales of Ancient Egypt* (1967; Puffin, 1987).

W.M. Flinders Petrie, *Amulets* (Constable & Co., London, 1914).

Frédéric Lionel, *The Magic Tarot* (Routledge, 1982).

Chapter 18

The Jewels of the Gods and the Insatiable Sea

(Middle East: Ancient Egypt)

There was a time when a goddess sat by the shores of the sea and heard its voice. It was angry and complained that the tribute it had received of silver, gold, lapis lazuli, and turquoise was not enough.

In its anger it flung the boxes of precious things upon the shore and raged into the streets of the towns.

The goddess went before the Council of the Ennead, the nine gods who ruled the earth from the City of the Sun. She spoke to Atum, the Father, to Shu the god of air, to Tefnut the goddess of water, to Geb the earth-god, and Nut the goddess of the sky. She spoke to their children – Osiris, Isis, Seth and Nepthys. All listened to the complaint of the sea and witnessed its raging on the shore, its incursion into the land.

"Let us give more gifts," they said. "Let us satisfy the sea."

Then Nut untied the necklace at her throat, the shining stars. Geb offered up his signet ring mined in the deepest caverns of the earth. Each offered up the jewels that adorned their forms – the secret, precious treasures of their hearts.

Servants came with baskets and carried all these things to the sea.

The sea reached out and took them. The sea was satisfied.

Comment

The story as told in *The Literature of Ancient Egypt* is fragmentary and very ancient, the same theme appearing in Canaanite legend as well as in Egyptian.

It can be interpreted in several ways. The one I favour is this: The sea represents the primeval source of all things. In most mythologies such a source is symbolized by the primeval waters of a great ocean. In Egyptian mythology it certainly is.

The "sea" is trying to indicate that even if you are a god or a goddess you must never forget that you came into existence only after the ocean. "The jewelry you wear marks your status in the divine hierarchy – but I was before you and without me you would not exist." As all things came from the sea, the sea can demand any thing it wishes back at any time. This must not be forgotten.

It is significant that the sea (the ultimate Deity) is not satisfied with any old boxes of treasure, however valuable in monetary terms. What it demands is the personal and private sacrifice of the individual. The personal attention and respect of the individual.

Source

William Kelly Simpson (ed), The Literature of Ancient Egypt (Yale University Press, 1972), pp. 133–6.

Chapter 19

The Turquoise Pendant

(Middle East: Ancient Egypt)

The tradition is that Prince Khafra related the following story to his father, King Khufu, about King Sneferu, his grandfather.

Sneferu was bored and depressed one day and asked his chief scribe, Djadjaemankh, what he could suggest to make the time pass more pleasantly. The scribe suggested the king go boating on the lake with the prettiest girls that could be found.

The king set off in a boat with the scribe, and twenty beautiful young girls dressed only in loosely woven net. They sang as they rowed the boat with ebony oars decorated with gold. Water birds flew up ahead of them, flowering reeds shook in the breeze, and sunlight and shade flickered through the leaves of the tall palms that lined the shore.

As he watched their beautiful bodies moving in rhythm King Sneferu began to smile, his boredom and depression forgotten.

But suddenly there was a commotion from the stern of the boat and the girls stopped rowing. He demanded to know what was happening.

It seemed that the turquoise pendant worn by one of the girls had fallen into the water and was lost. She was weeping and splashing about with her arms trying to recover it. Some of the others were trying to prevent her falling in.

When the king heard what the trouble was he at once said he would replace the jewel and that she must think no more about it. But this did not quieten her and she insisted that no jewel could replace the one she had lost and they should all help her to try to recover it.

"My Majesty," she said, "it is no ordinary jewel. It is green turquoise of the most precious kind, a fish talisman against drowning. My Majesty's father gave it to my mother's mother and it is of great value to me. Without it who knows what harm will come to me." The young woman was distraught and could not be comforted. All the joy had gone out of the afternoon for her and for her companions – all of whom understood how a talisman as precious as that, especially one that has been handed down through many generations, should be recovered at all costs.

The king turned to his chief scribe, a man known to be a powerful magician, a man who had learned the inner meaning of words from the god Djehuti himself.

"Djadjaemankh," he said, "this is a challenge for you. See if you can meet it."

Djadjaemankh agreed to try, but insisted that they return to the shore. When they had disembarked he stood alone at the edge of the lake, his hands held before him, his lips murmuring the words of a secret spell, his eyes closed. Silently the others watched and waited until they felt a strangeness about the air, a tingling in their bodies, their hearts beating faster in anticipation of something strange and possibly fearful about to happen.

And then they saw a ripple in the water moving to the centre of the lake. It was as though there were a fish swimming in a straight line, its fin cutting the water.

And then the watchers gasped, for it seemed the invisible fin had indeed cut the water, and behind it the waters were parting neatly so that a dry passage appeared and the bottom of the lake was revealed.

Then Djadjaemankh stepped forward and walked calmly between the two shining walls of water until he reached the turquoise pendant. They saw him stoop down and pick it up. They saw him turn and walk back.

When he was on the shore again he made a sign with his hands and murmured the conclusion of the spell. Instantly the walls of water broke and the two halves of the lake flowed together again, their meeting throwing up such a wave that all on shore were inundated up to their waists.

"Ah, Djadjaemankh," King Sneferu cried. "You are indeed a man of power worthy of your reputation."

With a bow and a smile the scribe gave the jewel to the king, who in turn placed it on the young girl's neck.

Comment

Turquoise was mined in the Sinai and was highly prized by the Egyptians. The earliest mines were in granite and very difficult to work with copper and flint tools. The men lived in an arid and inhospitable land and suffered greatly. Chapels to Hathor, the protective "Lady of the Turquoise", and Wepawet, the Opener of the Ways, have been found by archaeologists. The Egyptians discovered the whereabouts of the veins by following the wandering Bedouin, or "sand-dwellers", who had been trading beads of turquoise since very early times. The "Terraces of Turquoise" were the primary reason for the Egyptians originally going to the Sinai. So precious was it to the ancient Egyptians that they invented turquoise-coloured faience out of crushed quartz, the richest, purest turquoise kept exclusively for the Pharaoh and his favourites. No wonder the young girl in the boat was desolate when she lost her pendant. But even when the king offered to replace it for her she was not comforted. The turquoise pendant may have been valuable in the material sense, but it was far more valuable to her as an object imbued with magic.

The parting of the waters by the magician is particularly interesting to us in the light of the parting of the Red Sea for Moses (trained in Egyptian magic while he was living as a royal prince).

Symbolically, the great lake (or ocean) of consciousness is "parted" for some jewel of great significance to be found, or for some people to escape from the bondage of the senses into the freedom of the Spiritual Realms. Put another way, in order for us to see and obtain the "spiritual" life, we have to make a clear passage through our ordinary consciousness, we have to push back our normal consciousness in a way that seems impossible and see what is hidden beneath it,

The Pharaoh Sneferu is bored with his ordinary life. He is ready for an adventure. He starts with the sensual pleasure of watching the semi-naked girls and is jolted by some untoward accident or design on the part of the magician, the mentor, into an adventure with deeper implications. He learns that he can, as Pharaoh, obtain the precious jewel turquoise, but not the significance that the talisman has for the young girl. He learns that *that* can only he found by bending the normal rules of reality, and seeking it by paranormal means. "Paranormal" in this context suggests the use of mind over matter, spirit over body.

Source

C. Jacq, *Egyptian Magic*, translated by J. M. Davis (Aris & Phillips, 1985), pp. 90–1.

Donald A. Mackenzie, *Egyptian Myth and Legend* (The Gresham Publishing Co., London), pp. 144–5.

William Kelly Simpson (ed.), *The Literature of Ancient Egypt* (Yale University Press, 1972).

Chapter 20

Moses and the Sapphire Tablets

(Middle East)

In the third month the twelve tribes made camp at the foot of a high mountain. Behind them stretched the wilderness. Before them and on either side stretched the wilderness. It seemed to them it was more harsh than their taskmasters in Egypt, more cruel than Pharaoh himself. Many murmured against Moses, as many had murmured before. There was bitterness in the twelve tribes, restlessness, despair. The bare land yielded very little for their flocks and herds to eat. The manna that had fallen from heaven was long gone. The water that Moses had miraculously produced out of a dry rock had been long since drunk. The column of smoke by day and the column of fire by night which Moses said the Lord had sent to lead them to the Promised Land, no longer awed them. Some said it was no more than yet another of the magic tricks of which Moses, as a trained Egyptian priest, was capable.

Moses began to climb the mountain. He was exhausted. For month after month, he had carried the burden of their doubt, their resentment, their longing to return to the Egypt they knew and abandon the quest for the Promised Land they did not know. Many had died on the way. Many were sick. He looked back and saw as far as the eye could see the brown goat-hair tents, the skeletal cattle searching for thorn bushes, the dispirited people clustered in groups. It seemed a long time since he had had a sign from God. He himself was on the verge of doubting. Even the spectacular parting of the waters that had allowed his people to pass to safety, might have been some extraordinary aberration of Nature, coincidental with their need to escape.

Even the plagues that had driven Pharaoh at last to let them go could be explained. True, it was unusual for so many disasters to befall a country in such quick succession – but it was not impossible.

Moses turned his back wearily on his people and continued to climb the mountain, longing for solitude away from the continual jabber of voices, the continual demands on his time and his strength.

"What if I was wrong?" he thought. "What if all the signs I have received, the voices I have heard, were false? What if all the promises were given by an evil spirit – not the great I AM, the Being before all beings? What if I am leading my people towards millennia of suffering instead of to freedom?"

The rock was burning hot under his hands and his sandalled feet. The sky was immeasurably vast and high.

"I will not come down," he vowed, "until I have found the Truth."

He reached the summit and he bowed to the ground.

He remained there for a long time in silence.

No sound, not even an eagle's cry, broke the stillness of the air. It was as though he were alone in the world – the last or the first man on earth.

And then into that silence thoughts began to crowd – thoughts over which he had no control, thoughts that were not his own.

"Now, therefore, if ye will obey my voice indeed, and keep my covenant, then ye shall be a peculiar treasure unto me above all people: for all the earth is mine" (Exodus 19:5).

The man rose up and looked around. The world lay at his feet from horizon to horizon. The sun, the great Eye, stared down at him. But the conviction of his heart had changed. *If* a people, his people, kept the faith and obeyed the commands of the Almighty God, surely the Great Design would unfold as it was intended, and all would be well. But if they deformed and despoiled the work, trying to impose their own limited vision on it – all would not by any means be well.

This he felt at last was Truth.

With a light heart he came down from the mountain and

called the Elders of the people to him. He told them that he had spoken with the Lord, and the Lord had told him how he would protect the people who obeyed his commands and how he would reward them. The message was passed on by the Elders to the people, and the people eagerly vowed to obey the Lord in every way.

Confidently Moses climbed the mountain again to take this message from the people back to the Lord; but he knew in his heart that saying is one thing, and doing is another. It is easy to believe at one moment and doubt at another. When he came down again he brought the message that if the people would cleanse and purify themselves thoroughly, on the third day of purification the Lord himself would appear to them on the mountain.

The preparations and purifications were done in good spirit, and on the third day a huge throng gathered around the base of the mountain. Moses set bounds around the base and warned the people that anyone who overstepped those bounds would be put to death.

The people waited nervously. They were hungry, for they had fasted; they were tired, for they had prayed all night; and they were afraid, for they were about to see God.

Moses stood ahead of them looking up to the summit of the mountain.

And then they felt the earth tremble beneath their feet, and a rock or two fell from the cliffs and crashed into the valley. Smoke rose from the summit, and thunder and lightning played about them. Terrified they clung together. And then they heard the sound of a mighty trumpet blasting out time and again. Moses spoke, and a voice seemed to answer from the swirling cloud, calling him to come to the summit.

He left the people, disappearing into the cloud, but returned soon after to charge them once again, on pain of death, not to set foot on the mountain.

When the people heard the thunder and saw the lightning, and the black clouds swirling, and heard the eerie trumpet sound coming from within them, they drew back and told Moses to speak with God for them. They were too afraid to commune with him direct.

So "the people stood afar off, and Moses drew near unto the thick darkness where God was".

When he returned he stood on a high rock and told the people the Lord had commanded that they build no elaborate altars for sacrifice, but treat the earth itself as a sacred altar. He promised them an angel as a protector and a guide to lead them in the ways of righteousness. The people listened, but many things he said were not understood.

Then Moses spelled out laws and judgements for them. After this, detail by detail, he told them how they were to treat their cattle, their servants, their relations, their friends. He spoke of judgements and retribution, of compensation for wrongs done, of tithes and taxes to be paid. He promised them that the Lord had prepared a land for them and would help them to destroy all the people presently occupying it, so that it would be theirs for generation after generation.

The people listened. The people believed the Lord God was speaking to them through the mouth of their leader, Moses.

All these things Moses wrote down so that his people would not forget them. He read the words he had written aloud, and the people agreed to abide by the rules.

He built an altar with twelve pillars, each pillar to represent one of the tribes of Israel. On this altar he made sacrifice, and the blood of the sacrifice he sprinkled upon the tribes that they would be bound by blood to this covenant.

Then he and his brother Aaron, his brother's sons, Nadab and Abihu, and seventy of the Elders of Israel began to climb the mountain. Suddenly they had a vision of the God of Israel standing on a pavement of sapphire as clear as heaven. (Exodus 24: 10: "And they saw the God of Israel: and there was under his feet as it were a paved work of a sapphire stone, and as it were the body of heaven in his clearness.")

Moses and Joshua climbed higher, charging the Elders to stay where they were and to look to Aaron and Hur if they needed any guidance.

The cloud came down thick around the summit and Moses disappeared from view.

The Elders waited and waited and eventually returned to the people. Forty days and forty nights went by and there was no sign of Moses. Upon the summit fire was raging, smoke billowing. The people began to murmur that Moses had been consumed by his God and they were mad to have trusted such a deity. They longed for the gods of Egypt who seemed easier to understand, and they made a golden image of the Apis Bull the Egyptians sanctified. And they worshipped it.

Moses came down from the mountain carrying two tablets of sapphire crystal, inscribed on both sides – the tablets the work of God, and the writing the writing of God.

But when Moses drew near the base of the mountain and the camp of the Israelites he could hear their profane prayers and see what god they had set up for themselves.

In a rage he raised the tablets above his head and smashed them to the ground. Splinters of sapphire spread far and wide and the writing of God was lost to man forever.

Then Moses raged through the camp and punished them for what they had done, telling them what vengeance God would take against them for their profanity. But with God he pleaded for mercy and, at last, when he had built the sanctuary, the tabernacle, and the Ark and the Covenant, exactly as he believed it should be from his communion with God on top of the mountain, he told them God had softened his heart towards his people.

Moses returned once more to the summit alone, and again stayed for forty days and forty nights. He took stone and himself inscribed two tablets of law and judgement of the people. These we know as the Ten Commandments. They were carved by Moses – not by God. To this day no one knows what was written on the original sapphire tablets by God's own hand, though many mystics have sought to find out by prayer and meditation.

Comment

That Moses and Aaron and Aaron's two sons and the seventy Elders saw God standing on a pavement of sapphire (Exodus 24:9) gave rise to the legend that the first two tablets of stone, the ones inscribed by God himself, were of sapphire. It seemed logical that God (if he was being imaged in human form) would stoop down and pick up the stone nearest to himself.

In *The Secret Teachings of all Ages* (p. xcviii) Manly P. Hall writes:

> *While upon the heights of Mount Sinai, Moses received from Jehovah two tablets bearing the characters of the Decalogue traced by the very finger of Israel's God. These tablets were fashioned from the divine sapphire, Schethuyâ, which the Most High, after removing from His own throne, had cast into the Abyss to become the foundation and generation of the worlds. This sacred stone, formed of heavenly dew, was sundered by the breath of God, and upon the two parts were drawn in black fire the figures of the Law. These precious inscriptions, aglow with celestial splendour, were delivered by the Lord on the Sabbath day into the hands of Moses, who was able to read the illumined letters from the reverse side because of the transparency of the great jewel.*

Manly Hall says we may read the details of this legend in the *Zohar*, the "Secret Doctrine of Israel".

Manly Hall continues:

> *Because of the idolatry of the Israelites, Moses deemed the people unworthy to receive the sapphire tablets; hence he destroyed them, that the Mysteries of Jehovah should not be violated...The blazing light of the divine word was*

lost...leaving only its shadow with the children of the twelve tribes.

Z'ev ben Shimon Halevi mentions another version of the legend of the destruction of the first tablets in his book *Kabbalah and Exodus*. In this version Moses turns back when he realizes the Israelites have chosen to worship a physical representation of the Ineffable, "but the seventy Elders pursued him to take possession of the wondrous tablets. As he miraculously flew before them he saw the Divine Words vanish from the Tablets and they became so unbearably heavy that they fell to earth and were shattered."

Centuries of speculation have followed as to what exactly was written on the sapphire tablets, and several esoteric schools believe that they have the answer.

According to Gershom Scholem in his book *On the Kabbalah and Its Symbolism*, a certain school of Kabbalists "started with the old conception that the souls of Israel who went out of Egypt and received the Torah at Mount Sinai numbered 600,000. According to the laws of transmigration and the distribution of the sparks into which the soul disintegrates, these 600,000 primordial souls are present in every generation of Israel... "Consequently, there are 600,000 aspects and meanings in the Torah. According to each one of these ways of explaining the Torah, the root of a soul has been fashioned in Israel. In the Messianic age, every single man in Israel will read the Torah in accordance with the meaning peculiar to his root. And thus also is the Torah understood in Paradise" (Isaac Luria)... Menahem Azariah of Fano, of the great Italian Kabbalists (c.1600) says in this treatise on the soul that the Torah as originally engraved on the first tablets (those that were broken) contained these 600,000 letters [or roots] and that only on the second tablets did it assume its shorter form..."

Some believe God's tablets revealed the eternal truths from the Tree of Life, later systematized by the Kabbalists as the mystic Sephiroth, and that the later tablets inscribed by Moses "revealed only temporal truths from the Tree of Knowledge".

Manly Hall tells us that the ten spheres of the Tree of Life (the ten sephiroth) "were called the shining sapphires, and it is believed by many Rabbis that the word sapphire is the basis of the word Sephira (the singular of sephiroth)".

The wisdom of the Kabbalists is immensely subtle and complex and even after a lifetime's study is probably well beyond the reach of most people. The modern Western writer who has made many of its essential teachings intelligible to me is Z'ev ben Shimon Halevi (Warren Kenton). In a series of brilliant and accessible books he describes something of the mystical meaning of the Tree of Life of the Kabbalists. He shows us that sentences we might have read in the Bible have a significance far beyond what we first thought. For instance the apparent repetition in Isaiah 43:7 is not repetition at all:

"Even every one that is called by My Name, for I have created him for my Glory, I have formed him; yea I have made him." Halevi says "These four levels of calling, creating, forming and making recur throughout the Scriptures and throughout Kabbalah." The calling is associated with pure Divine Will, creating is associated with Divine Intellect, forming with Divine Emotion, and making with Divine Action.

"Creation in this particular Kabbalist scheme begins in being willed or called forth by I AM THAT I AM. The second stage is one of pure Idea; in the third the idea manifests in Form; in the fourth it is set in motion, and in reacting with other forms becomes part of an ever-changing pattern – the universe we know."

Each of these stages corresponds to a "realm", and each realm has an elaborate dynamic of its own. From Ain Soph, "the eternal state of Being, the Incomprehensible First Principle or Supreme Deity, an instantaneous and powerful surge of energy zig zags down through the Tree of Life, an arrangement of ten spheres or sephira" represented by a central trunk of equilibrium, flanked by positive and negative, active and passive, "with an eleventh undefined, mysterious sphere in which the Holy Spirit hovers unmanifested, ever present and unconfined" (Manly Hall). The Matthews, in *The Western Way*, called the ten sephira "the ten essences of God's emanation".

In my novel *The Tower and the Emerald* I made an attempt to describe The Tree of Life:

> *...but the natural living tree before her began to take on a visionary quality. It became for her the mysterious Tree of Life, reaching up through all the Realms of Being to the very borders of that region where not even the archangels dare penetrate...*
>
> *She realized that the Tree was growing as much downwards from above, as though rooted in the Light of Heaven, as it was growing upwards from below, where it was rooted in the World of Changes, the World of Matter.*
>
> *She saw herself as Spirit from the highest realms, rooted now in the earth, but striving to return. She saw around her the world of air, earth, fire and water: the multitudinous beings of the World of Matter: and above her she saw the non-material World of the Soul, the region of angels and of demons, of elementals and of those who are awaiting rebirth. She knew that beyond this there were other realms, still out of reach of her understanding even in her most inspired moments: the Realm of pure Spirit where the mighty archangels observe and act – known as "the gods' to pagans – even they still far from the threshold of the Unknown, the Dwelling of the Nameless One.*
>
> *She envisaged the Tree with energy flowing up and down from the First to the Last, the One to the Many, and back again. She saw spheres and realms contained within the Tree, each with its precise meaning and function. She saw beings going up and down and up again, animated by the tremendous "lightning flash" of God's desire for life, yet freely motivated by their own longing to explore before their yearning to rejoin their source drove them back, transformed and enriched.*
>
> *She saw those who rose and those who fell. She saw those who tried and tried again, and those embittered and failed beings who had given up trying...*

Whether the Kabbalists' scheme is close to what God wrote on those first sapphire tablets or not we do not know. I have sometimes dreamed of writing a novel in which three archaeologists, one Jewish, one Christian, one Islamic, set off for the Sinai desert to search for the fragments of the sapphire tablets, each with his or her own idea of what will be found written on them. It would be interesting if each located some of the fragments and, in the end, they were forced to co-operate with each other because the fragments could not be deciphered unless they were put together. And it would be even more interesting if – when the pieces are finally put together again – each of the religions discover to their amazement that they do not say at all what they have been teaching all these centuries.

I am reminded of the Hopi legend of the two brothers. They are each given a tablet of stone by the Great Spirit on which there is writing. When they complain that they can't read the writing, the Great Spirit tells them that they must separate. The one brother must remain on the ancestral lands and keep the ancestral wisdom alive. The other must travel across the world, learning all he can from his experience and from other cultures. When he returns they must put the two tablets together and only then will they be able to read them.

I sometimes muse that certain of the smallest fragments might have, in flying far and wide, entered the hearts of certain people, as the splinters of ice did in the Hans Andersen legend of the Snow Queen. Perhaps the great sages and prophets, the saints and bodhisattvas, receive by mystical means such splinters of God's original teaching as they are capable of absorbing and the great sapphire tablets are not completely lost after all.

It may be that a fragment or two might have been found in ancient times, and lost again – still existing somewhere for us to rediscover.

There is a legend that there was once a great sapphire above the altar at Glastonbury Abbey at the height of its glory – a sapphire that had been brought from Jerusalem by St David. Geoffrey Ashe in *King Arthur's Avalon* mentions the great sapphire of St David found at Glastonbury at the time of the Norman abbot Henry de Blois (1126) in a cupboard where it had been hidden for safe keeping during the Danish invasions.

During the time of Walter Masington (1342–75) the sapphire was suspended above the altar, only to be lost again in 1539 when Glastonbury Abbey was despoiled by the agents of Henry VIII.

That it was brought from Jerusalem is very significant. Could it have been one of the fragments picked up by Moses or one of the Israelites at the foot of Mount Sinai, brought to the Holy Land as a sacred relic, installed in Solomon's Temple, hidden during its destruction, and passed secretly and reverently from keeper to keeper until it came into St David's hands at last? Might it not still be in Britain? Might it not be one of our crown jewels? Might it not be exhibited in some museum, not even the curator knowing its true significance? Perhaps it is in private hands, or is sunk in some marsh or buried for protection in some remote place? The search for it could be an adventure of a physical nature or a spiritual one. What did God really write on those tablets? The search in itself would surely be rewarding – as the Kabbalists have already discovered.

"The *Zohar* is a congeries of treatises, texts, extracts or fragments of texts, belonging to different periods, but all resembling one another in their method of mystical interpretation of the Torah...It is the fundamental book of Jewish Cabbalism. It is the premier textbook of medieval Jewish mysticism..." (J. Abelson, 1931, from his introduction to the *Zohar* translated by Harry Sperling, Maurice Simon, and Dr Paul P. Levertoff).

I searched the *Zohar* for references to the sapphire tablets and was excited to find the following passages in Volume III:

... the Divine Word descended from heaven ... and impressed itself upon the tablets of stone, until the whole Ten Words were designed thereon ... every word contained all manner of legal implications and derivations, as well as all mysteries and hidden aspects; for each word was indeed like unto a treasure-house, full of all precious things. And though when one Word was uttered it sounded but as itself, yet when it was stamped upon the stone

seventy different aspects were revealed in it ... And every one according to his grade saw and received the Words. (p.251)

"When the letters were engraved upon the two tablets of stone they were visible on both sides of the tablets. The tablets were of sapphire stone, and the letters were formed of white fire and covered again with black fire, and were engraved upon both sides." Another authority said "the tablets were not engraved but the letters fluttered on to them, being visible in two colours of fire, white and black...white for Mercy, black for Power and Severity." (p.254)

It is written "And the tablets were the work of God" (Ex. 22, 18) ... They were originally two sapphire stones which were rough-hewn, but the Holy One caused a wind to blow upon them, which smoothed them and transformed them into two tablets.

These two tablets existed from before Creation, but were perfected on the sixth day of Creation specially for this purpose; thus they were a special creation of the Holy One. (p.255)

The Ten Words contain the essence of all the commandments, the essence of all celestial and terrestrial mysteries, the essence of the Ten Words of Creation. They were engraved on tablets of stone and all the hidden things were seen by the eyes and perceived by the minds of Israel, everything being made clear to them. At that house all the mysteries of the Torah, all the hidden things of heaven and earth, were unfolded before them and revealed...for they saw eye to eye the splendour of the glory of their Lord. (p.280)

When Moses broke the tablets "under the mountain; (Ex.

*32, 19), the Ocean overflowed its borders and was on the
point of inundating the whole world. When Moses saw
how the waves were rising and threatening to overwhelm
the universe, straightway he "took the calf which they had
made and burnt it in the fire, and ground it to powder, and
strewed it upon the water" (Ex. 32, 20). Then he stationed
himself before the waters of the Ocean and said: "Waters,
waters, what would ye?" And they answered: "Was not
the world established by and on the merit of the Holy
Words engraved upon the tablets? And now, because the
Israelites have denied the Torah by making the golden
calf, we desire to overwhelm the world." (p.339)*

*Had not the tablets been broken, the world would not have
suffered as it subsequently did, and the Israelites would
have been in the likeness of the supernal angels above.
Therefore the Scripture proclaims: "the tablets were the
work of God" (Elohim), from the time when the world was
still under the aegis of the name Elohim, before the
Sabbath had entered. The writing, too, was the "writing of
God", black fire on white fire, and it was engraved
because the Jubilee proclaims freedom to all worlds.
(pp.339–40)*

*"And under His feet as it were a paved work of a sapphire
stone" – what was this which they saw? They beheld the
precious stone with which the Holy One will build the
future Sanctuary, as it is written: "I will lay thy stones
with fair colours and lay thy foundations with sapphires'
(Isa. LIV, II). (p.356)*

*The colour purple-blue symbolizes the throne of God.
"And above the firmament... was the likeness of a throne,
as the appearance of a sapphire stone... and it had
brightness round about" (Ezek. 1, 26–27). (p.399)*

Day unto day, grade unto grade, in order that the one

175

should complete itself in the other, and one be illumined
by the other from the luminous and sparkling radiance of
the Sapphire which is reflected by the heavens back to the
central glory. (p.391)

Sources

The Bible: Exodus chapters 19–24, 32.

Manly P. Hall, *The Secret Teachings of all Ages* (1901; The Philosophical Research Society, Inc., Los Angeles, 1977).

John and Caitlin Matthews, *The Western Way* (Arkana, 1986), Vol. II.

Geoffrey Ashe, *King Arthur's Avalon* (Fontana, 1957).

Z'ev ben Shimon Halevi, *A Kabbalistic Universe* (Rider, 1977).

——, *Kabbalah and Exodus* (Rider, 1980).

——, *Kabbalah: Tradition of Hidden Knowledge* (Thames & Hudson, 1979).

Gershom Scholem, *On the Kabbalah and Its Symbolism* (Schocken Books, New York, 1965).

The Zohar, translated by Harry Sperling, Maurice Simon, and Dr Paul P. Levertoff (The Soncino Press, 1970).

Chapter 21

Shey, the Crystal Mountain

(Far East)

In Nepal, bordering Tibet, in the remote mountainous district of Dolpo, north of the Himalayas, there is a sacred mountain called Shey, which translated means "crystal".

The legend of how it became crystal and how it became sacred is well known to both the valley farmers and the nomad Yak herders of the high pastures, but not to city-dwellers far from the pillars of the world, the sacred mountains.

In the ancient days the mountain was the abode of fierce gods, gods of storm and earthquake – violent, unforgiving, powerful. The people believed they held on to their precarious existence only at the whim of these gods, and much of their time was spent in pleading with them for protection and propitiating them with gifts they could ill afford.

One day a Buddhist monk, Drutob Senge Yeshe, came that way and was saddened to see the people's fearful and crippling dependence on animist spirits. No time was spent in seeking enlightenment, only on subsistence and physical survival. He tried to teach them the principles of the Buddhist belief that the material world is of little consequence, and that the development and training of their own inner spiritual reality would transcend all other activities. But the concept was too abstract, too intellectual for them.

Drutob Senge Yeshe then climbed the mountain that was the abode of the god they most feared and sat upon its summit in deep meditation.

The story of what happened then is still told around the hearth fires of Dolpo.

Riding on a snow lion Drutob Senge Yeshe went out to meet the fierce mountain god. He sought him among harsh crags of dark rock. He sought him in the black and dangerous clouds that swirled around the summit. The god flung spears of lightning. The snow lion dodged. The god intensified his attack and the iron rocks were alive with dangerous electrical charges. The snow lion took to the air and bravely flew into the heart of the storm. The god filled the clouds with hissing serpents. The snow lion burst open and released 108 manifestations of itself to fight the serpents.

On his back the monk chanted the sacred words and meditated on eternal truths.

One by one the snow lions overcame the serpents. The deafening drumming thunder died down; the energy of lightning weakened until it was no more than an occasional fitful glow.

From the heavens descended a white conch shell. The holy man took it in his hand and blew it. The sound reverberated through the rocks, the deep and sustained resonance bringing about transformation. The abode of the dark earth spirit became pure crystal. He could no longer hide and spring out to harm the people. He could no longer brood and sulk. Light had penetrated his secret lair. Light had reached his heart.

Drutob Senge Yeshe came out of deep meditation and looked around him. Water sang through the white crevices and flowed joyfully to the lake in the valley. Sunlight gleamed off the peaks. In an unbelievably blue sky a rainbow arched. The people would no longer fear the mountain and its guardian. The crystal mountain became a place of pilgrimage, of renewal, of enlightenment. Those who could not journey solely in high spirit-form like the sages, could yet climb the sacred crystal mountain with reverence and humility, putting themselves in the way of transcendent experience.

Comment

Not many Westerners have ever visited this remote place on Nepal's frontier with Tibet, but in the 1970s a young American, Joel F. Ziskin, did. He walked the pilgrim route to Shey, particularly interested, as a scholar, in the turning point when ancient animist beliefs gave way to the clarity and spirituality of the Buddhist tradition. In the legend of the Crystal Mountain he felt he had found the historical moment recorded, the moment when a Buddhist ascetic came to these mountains and converted the people with a story they could understand, a story of the age-old battle of good and evil personified as snow-white living lions and writhing serpent beings. The Buddhist symbol of the lion indicates spiritual zeal, the defender of the law and wisdom of Buddha. "The lion's roar is Buddha's fearless teaching of the Dharma," says J. C. Cooper in *An Illustrated Encyclopaedia of Traditional Symbols*. It represents "valour, energy, strength". In writing about the symbolism of the serpent, Cooper says (among other things, for serpent symbolism is very complex): "The chthonic serpent manifests the aggressive powers of the gods of the underworld and darkness; it is..."master of the bowels of the earth"." At the centre of the Wheel of Existence "the snake represents anger" for the Buddhists.

History gives us only the broad outlines of the conversion. The reality is not as simple and clear-cut. The people of these mountains still practise exorcism over the sick, believing that they have been possessed by an evil spirit. "The ancient gods still play an active part of the life of the people. If they did not, one wonders if it would be necessary to make the pilgrimage to Shey. Pilgrims are often seeking new confirmation for a belief that has been wavering, and forgiveness for a period of doubt. Standing in the rarefied atmosphere of the high peaks of the Crystal Mountain after the arduous climb around and up, the pilgrims' hearts and souls and minds are in a better state to listen to the "still, small voice" of the Higher Consciousness.

All else has fallen away. Here there is a true silence. They return to the noisy world of ephemeral things renewed and strengthened.

I found it interesting in Ziskin's account of his own pilgrimage that when he tried to speak with the holy hermit, Tulku Tsewang, he was told that he must come back *after* his ascent of Shey.

Drutob Senge Yeshe himself ascended the mountain to meditate and so work on the spiritual plane after the body and the will had been exercised to the full in preparation. Moses *climbed* Mount Sinai to speak with God. To reach a state of spiritual readiness for enlightenment we must make a considerable personal effort. A sage works for years to perfect body and spirit in readiness for enlightenment.

When the hermit of Shey finally agreed to speak with Ziskin after the long and exhausting climb to the top of the Crystal Mountain, Ziskin learned that Shey itself was of no more importance than a mayfly. It was not the summit of the mountain that he had been sent to find, but his own Self that had been with him all along, unrecognized.

Today's pilgrims dance joyfully in the snowfields where the snow lions once fought their battle against the snake-beings. Pilgrims bow to the ground before the shrine of Drutob Senge Yeshe. Pilgrims lay faceted crystals from the sacred mountain at the feet of the images of Buddha on their village and family altars – crystals that help them to remember that enlightened beings do not fear.

What is this enlightenment that defeats fear which we seek at the top of the Crystal Mountain? According to the Buddhists:

Everything that arises passes away. The whole process of life, including thinking as the constant movement of consciousness, is characterised as constant flux. Nothing has real duration: everything is at every moment passing away or else is assigned to a new becoming. Life is not static, but dynamic, and all moments of existence are intermediate states, even between two different kinds of state in the process of transformation. To recognise the

changeable nature of the whole empirical world means to
see its deceptive insubstantiality. Thus, there opens up the
path to the unchangeable, the reality of the deathless,
which is identical with the knowledge of the perfected and
liberated.

Detlef Ingo Lauf, *Secret Doctrines of the Tibetan Book*
of the Dead, p.18

There are two possible attitudes to life, and every
individual can be said to base his life on a compromise
between them. On the one hand there is what we call the
pagan attitude, according to which the world is this
world... In contrast to this is the spiritual attitude,
according to which the real centre of the universe, the true
reason for living... is invisible and lies elsewhere; this
world is a place of transit only, and life is a testing period,
an ordeal to overcome, or an illusion... The doctrine of
Buddha, like that of Christ, belongs... to the second
category.

Fosco Maraini, *Secret Tibet,* p.66

The snow lion flies above the earth – white, pure, strong.
The serpent-beings rise from the depths of the earth, from the
storm clouds that are part of the earth cycle.

But it is the mediation of the Buddhist ascetic that conjures
them into being from the earth side and the spiritual side of his
own being. Like Christ he enacts on behalf of us the drama of
the battle of good and evil that is always going on within us,
the struggle between our attachment to the things of this earth
and our search for a more permanent and significant reality.

By climbing the Crystal Mountain we share symbolically in
his experience, which gives us confidence to achieve our own
victory over the same forces.

The white conch shell is the equivalent of the biblical trumpet – a stirring call to action. But more than that it is a powerful
transforming agent. If modern physicists are right in joining
with their ancient Buddhist predecessors in believing that ma-

terial reality is no more than invisible and immeasurable impulses of energy in constant motion, it is not inconceivable that a sound that sets up a specific vibration could transform one apparent type of matter into another. We are not so far from the "Word" that began all things. Quartz crystal in particular is known to have a specific vibrationary rate.

The rainbow has always been the symbol in myth of the end of battle, the promise of peace.

The crystal is transparent. No shadows can lurk and hide. We can see into it and we can see into ourselves.

Shey today on one level is a huge contorted mass of crystalline limestone rock, containing fossil shells from a time many millions of years ago when it was below an ancient ocean – an ocean which has ceased to exist as the Buddhists said it would.

On another level it is a challenge to the human spirit.

Sources

Joel F. Ziskin, "Trek to Nepal's Sacred Crystal Mountain", *National Geographic* Vol. 151, No. 4, April 1977.

J. C. Cooper, *An Illustrated Encyclopaedia of Traditional Symbols* (Thames & Hudson, 1978).

Detlef Ingo Lauf, *Secret Doctrines of the Tibetan Book of the Dead* (Shambhala, Boulder, Colorado, and London, 1977), p. 18.

Fosco Maraini, *Secret Tibet* (Reader's Union, London, 1954), p. 66.

Chapter 22

Caurangipa, the Limbless One

(Far East)

There once was a handsome young Indian prince, Caurangi. When he was twelve years old his mother died and his father, the king, married again – this time a woman much younger than himself. Caurangi had loved his mother very much, and on her deathbed she had charged him never to do evil, but always good.

One day when the king was away in his forest retreat meditating, the young woman was bored and wandered about the palace looking for something to do. She came upon the young prince and at once desired him. She sent a servant to him with an invitation to come to her in bed.

Shocked, the youth refused at once and the servant delivered the message back to her mistress. The young queen was furious. She paced about her chamber all day and she paced about her chamber all night, trying to think of ways to punish him for his scornful treatment of her. At last she called a servant to her and demanded that they take the boy out and kill him because he had insulted her. But the servants refused, saying that the prince was but a child and surely did not intend any insult to her no matter what he had said or done.

Frustrated and bitter she devised a plan to get her own way, and when her husband returned from his retreat he found all the furniture in her chamber flung about, her clothes torn, her hair dishevelled, and scratches on her body. Sobbing, she told him that his son had tried to rape her.

Enraged, the father denounced his son and ordered that he was to be taken into the remotest part of the forest where the tigers prowled, his arms and legs were to be cut off, and he was to be left to die. His wife insisted that the limbs were to be brought back to the palace to prove that the orders had indeed been carried out.

Weeping, the servants took the boy into the forest, and he overheard them arguing about which limbs of their own sons they would cut off in order to provide the legs and arms to show the queen. They could not bear to carry out the sentence on the young prince.

Caurangi told them that it would be an evil on his part to allow another to die or be harmed in his place, and insisted that they carry out his father's orders.

Very unwillingly, they did what they had been ordered to do. The only compromise they made was to take him beyond the forest and leave his limbless form propped up against a tree, not far from inhabited lands.

No sooner had they departed, with heavy hearts, than the yogin Minapa appeared before the dying boy. He offered to give him instructions in breathing techniques and other matters which would lead to his eventual healing. The boy gladly accepted and was given instruction into the Buddha nature and the nature of all things. His initiation and empowerment followed, and he was told to continue the practice of what he had been taught, until, Minapa said, he had mastered it all. Then his limbs would grow again.

Minapa told the boy his own story. It seems he had once been a poor fisherman and had been swallowed whole by a whale. As it chanced, the wife of the god Siva Mahadeva had persuaded her husband to teach her the secrets of yoga. He had finally agreed, but knowing that there is danger if teachings of such power are given to people who are not ready for them, he took her to a bower under the sea, away from everyone, to instruct her. Interested in what was going on the whale swam nearby, and every day the fisherman heard the instructions of Siva Mahadeva, while the wife, bored, nodded off to sleep. At last the god discovered his secret student and gave him initiation. For twelve years Minapa practised what he had been taught, remaining in the whale. After twelve years the whale was caught. The fisherman, believing that there was treasure in his belly because he weighed so heavy, cut him open. Out walked Minapa singing:

> *"The source of my magic is twofold:*
> *It arises from the good fortune that accrued*
> *From the virtue of my past lives,*
> *And also from my steady devotion*
> *To the great teachings I have heard.*
> *Ah, my friends, what a precious jewel*
> *Is one's own mind."*

(Keith Dowman, Masters of Enchantment, p. 31)

When he had initiated the bleeding youth Minapa strode off towards the village. Seeing a group of boys he asked which one would give up his time to care for the dying boy. Goraksa, reduced to becoming a herd boy since his father fell on hard times and could not afford his education, said at once that he would do so if Minapa would look after his herds while he was away. It was agreed.

Goraksa bathed and bound the bleeding limbs and cared for the boy, giving him half his own food every day.

For twelve years the young prince practised what he had been taught. For twelve years Goraksa looked after his body.

One night some merchants carrying treasure of gold and silver and precious stones chanced to bury it near the tree against which Caurangi was propped in deep meditation. They were thinking to hide it from robbers while they slept.

Suddenly they heard a voice from the darkness saying:

"Who goes there?"

Fearing it was a bandit the merchants answered at once that they were poor charcoal burners and what they were burying was only charcoal.

"So be it," said the voice.

They heard no more, but in the morning when they looked into their bags they found charcoal instead of the gold, silver, and precious stones.

Horrified, they prepared to flee the country, for the treasure had belonged to the king and he would be angry at its loss. But one of them had a thought and reminded them of the words that had been spoken the night before – how they had lied and how their bluff had been called.

"This must be the work of a Master of Enchantment," he said.

They retraced their steps to the tree near which they had buried the treasure, and found a limbless man propped up against its trunk. They told him what had happened and he looked at them in surprise.

"I must have spoken out of my deep meditation," he said, "for I have no recollection of the incident."

But then he suddenly remembered Minapa's words. When he had mastered the teaching, his limbs would grow again. He transformed the charcoal back into gold and silver and precious stones and sent the merchants on their way.

That day, the twelfth anniversary of his wounding, the twelfth anniversary of his initiation by Minapa, he prayed for the return of his limbs...and his limbs grew.

That evening when Goraksa returned to his charge with a bowl of food he was astonished to find him standing straight and tall.

As a reward for his faithful service to Caurangi, Goraksa was initiated and trained by Minapa until he too became a great Mahasiddha.

> *"Whatever your birth – high, middle, or low –*
> *Use the circumstances of your life*
> *To the fullest. Realize the flow*
> *Of karma is helping you reach your goal.*
> *I seized my chance for enlightenment*
> *In faithful service to Caurangi, the Limbless One."*

(Dowman, p. 53)

Comment

It has long been known that in the Far East, particularly in India, certain highly developed Masters of Yoga can achieve extraordinary control of their minds and their bodies. This cannot be learned at a class once a week fitted into a busy worldly schedule, or at a weekend course, but takes long years of dedication, discipline, and gruelling practice under the tutelage of a True Master. But once these individuals have passed a certain stage of the training they can perform miracles such as walking on fire unburned, appearing in places far from where their body is known to be, bringing about physical changes in material reality, healing, prophesying, levitating...

But the performance of miracles by the Mahasiddhas, the Masters of Enchantment, while it alerts the uninitiated to the fact that the nature of reality cannot be taken for granted and is probably very different from what they have been led to believe, is not what the Mahasiddha is aiming at. Mahamudra, or the enlightenment achieved by the Buddha himself, "the attainment of a sustained ultimate experience of the oneness of all things... the dissolution of the individual personality into the universal mind" (Dowman, p. 14), is really the crown of their efforts. The performance of miracles is a kind of secondary offshoot, a subsidiary phenomenon thrown up almost irrelevantly during the achievement of their primary concern.

Although the great days of the Mahasiddhas is thought to be over, the twelfth-century Tibetan manuscripts describing the lives of eighty-four Mahasiddhas considered to be a record of the past, there are still alive today a few who achieve what they achieved, and many who try. In India, in the Hindu tradition that took over from the Buddhists, there is Sai Baba who manifests solid objects and quantities of healing ash out of nowhere, and who appears in places impossible for him to be, but insists that these miracles are no more than his "calling cards' and that they are used only to shock us into taking notice of his teaching. "Look with the eyes of the soul." "Distinguish between illusion and reality." "Spiritual love is central, miracles are small items. Love is giving and forgiving." "Control of mind is essential in the spiritual approach, since mind can potentially create anything."

In the story of Caurangipa we have an example that is repeated time and again in the stories of the Mahasiddhas, of how the moment must be right for starting on the Path towards enlightenment, and when the moment is right the guru appears. It is worth noting that Caurangi's father had just returned from a period of meditation when he was deceived by his wife and pronounced a cruel punishment on his son. He might have thought he was meditating – but obviously he was not. False meditation is useless.

All three of the men in this story who eventually become Mahasiddhas had suffered some misfortune or shock which brought them to a crucial turning point in their lives. The familiar background to their lives was suddenly removed and they were faced with the choice of death and despair, or life and enlightenment. It is true that Goraksa's loss of worldly wealth and his having to take up the humble life of a herd boy was not as dramatic as losing all his limbs or being swallowed by a whale, but it served the same purpose.

The young Caurangi refuses the seduction of the evil queen. That is, he refuses to be part of the corrupt practices of the world. He is misunderstood by the world and all but destroyed by it. Because of the inner strength he has shown in rejecting both temptations – sexual gratification – and, even more seductive, life itself at the expense of another – the Upper World accepts him. One of the Holy Ones comes to him and offers to show him another way to live. He accepts. This again is a positive act of will. He rejected evil. He now accepts good. The Way he is given is not easy. For twelve years he has to practise certain meditative techniques that will bring his mind into tune with the Universal Mind, and master his own body. The fact that his own adversity gives another man, Goraksa, the opportunity to attain Buddha enlightenment, reminds us that all our acts, good or evil, rebound upon others.

The moment comes when Caurangi is finally ready to become whole again, the moment when he has totally transcended the body and can achieve siddhi. The different levels of his consciousness have separated out during his training so that he can be aware of different things simultaneously on different levels of reality. The coming together again of these levels of consciousness after the separation, into a new and enlightened whole, makes him capable of things he had never dreamed of before.

> *In the Chinese text* The Secret of the Golden Flower *it is said that the meditations reach a stage where consciousness is dissolved. This state, for which the meditating person in this Chinese Yoga practice has been watching, is a kind of conscious dissociation. The text says that literally every partial thought or representation becomes visible, the whole power of the soul shows its traces, The picture which accompanies this text... is that of a man sitting in the lotus position and from his head rises one Buddha after the other, so that he has a whole crowd of Buddhas, each Buddha again creating two more, and so on. There is an infinite multiplication of different Buddhas, all sitting in the lotus position. After this state of consciously reached dissociation, the next step is to reintegrate all these Buddhas by becoming aware of the so-called rotation of the light.*
>
> (Marie-Louise Von Franz, *Creation Myths*, p. 204)

I see this multiplication of Buddhas as an image describing the separate awareness in the individual of all the different levels of consciousness available to us. This "separate awareness' is a necessary stage before the experience of the Whole, the Oneness, the "Suchness", is achieved.

When this final state is reached Caurangi can transform jewels into charcoal and charcoal into jewels. I believe he actually did this as I believe Sai Baba today can do this kind of thing, and as I believe Christ turned the water into wine at the wedding of Cana. The energy of mind, soul, and spirit working together instead of pulling against one another is extraordinarily powerful. That his limbs grew again when he reached this state is quite conceivable to me, for, though I have not witnessed the actual growth of limbs on a limbless person, I have personally witnessed healing in which material changes have definitely happened when there has been nothing else to account for it but the intense concentration of prayer and/or psychic energy.

That jewels turn into charcoal and charcoal into jewels is most interesting on a purely scientific level. We all know that diamonds, for instance, are a form of carbon that has been changed by great heat and pressure into crystal. But whether the twelfth-century scribes who wrote this story down, or the ancient people who passed it on before it was written, knew that, is doubtful.

Though the transformation could have been literal, and I believe it was, the event is not meant to be interpreted purely literally. Caurangi has reached that state of enlightenment when there is no distinction between one thing and another. "This' and "that" no longer exist as separate entities but are subsumed into the One. He has attained "the dissolution of the individual personality into the universal mind" (Dowman). Charcoal and diamonds are all one to him and he regards them as interchangeable.

Also in a sense the treasure represents the worldly wealth of his father he no longer has. It may be that in the early years of his suffering he might have longed for this – but now he has no wish for it. Charcoal that gives heat to a cold and lonely man is worth more than all the gold and silver and precious stones of the king.

We are not told in this story what happened to the merchants after this incident. I wouldn't be surprised if they too began to question reality – particularly the one who had the perspicacity to realize that the transformation had occurred to teach them a lesson and was the work of a Mahasiddha.

Sources

Masters of Enchantment: The Lives and Legends of the Mahasiddhas translated by Keith Dowman (Arkana, 1988).

Marie-Louise Von Franz, *Creation Myths* (Spring Publications, Dallas, Texas, 1983; distributed in the UK by Element Books), p. 204.

Chapter 23

Atlantis

One: The Destruction

The High Priest My-or trod carefully on the polished silver stairs – the crystal columns beside him reflecting in the mirror surface. This might be the last time he officiated at the divination service. Twice he had read the auguries for disaster and twice he had been reprimanded by the king, that stupid man, unfit to be a slave, let alone a king. He had been warned that if he did not retract his prophecy he might not live to leave the Temple. The rumour had spread that something momentous was about to happen and the throng that lined the way to the Temple was restless and anxious. Apart from the inner council of priests and royalty no one knew exactly what he had seen on the surface of the water.

The crowds were left behind. No one climbed these silver steps but the priesthood and the royal family. At the top, in the hall of mirrors, he could see his colleagues waiting. They knew. They knew what he had said he'd seen, and what the king's reaction to it had been. Some of the faces were hard and bitterly gleeful – praying that he would not retract and that he would be destroyed. Less corrupt than most of them, he had never been popular. Others, who respected him, watched anxiously – dreading that what he had seen would be confirmed, and yet dreading that it would not. If what he saw was a true foretelling, they were all doomed, not only he. And if it was not, they would have to distrust the oracle and this would entail a radical rethinking of all that they believed about the nature of reality.

The hall had mirrors on the floor, the ceiling, the walls, and on the columns that formed an alternating double circle. It was impossible to tell the numbers of those who waited in the hall just by looking, for the mirror surfaces were so pure and clean that even when their images were reflected back and forth a third or fourth time the reflections could not be distinguished from the reality.

He stepped among them, his image multiplying as he walked steadily through the hall. No one who was not part of the inner council would ever be able to find the door. The room was a cube of apparently undivided mirror. Sometimes novices had gone mad in this hall, tormented by echoing and mocking images, unable to tell the difference between illusion and reality, believing it impossible to find the way out, all sense of orientation and selfhood gone.

My-or glanced over his shoulder. The door through which he had come had disappeared. The wall behind him was as apparently solid and unbroken as those at the two sides and ahead of him.

Long years of training had taught him not to rely on outward and visible signs but to use the crystals that had been implanted in his body and to recognize their subtle and almost imperceptible resonance in reaction to other crystals within the Temple.

He found the door immediately and touched it with the large sapphire that was in the ring on his finger. It opened silently and he and the other priests detached themselves from their reflections and flowed into the adjoining chamber.

This was as dark as the other had been light. The walls and floor and ceiling were polished fine-grained black basalt. Seven steps of black obsidian led up to a plinth of jet on which was balanced a bowl of flawless rock-crystal filled with pure and tranquil water. The only light source in the room was inside the column of jet and shone up through the crystal bowl, making its translucence luminous. It was light floating in darkness like the moon in the night sky.

Silently his companions took their stand at even intervals

around the walls. There were ten of them, each representing one of the ten kingdoms of Atlantis, the ten kingdoms that had been handed down through generation after generation from the initial five sets of twins fathered on an earth-woman by the god Poseidon. He was the eleventh, the high priest, supposed to be answerable to no one but the god. But, here he was, under the command of a petty tyrant, expected to perjure his soul and lie.

The last two times he had looked into the crystal bowl such images had arisen in his mind he had been hard put to it not to run screaming from the place. He had seen the sky on fire and the mountains and forest and cities of his land hurled hither and thither in a mighty cataclysm. He had seen walls of ocean water a mile high crashing down on this very chamber.

The first time he had fainted, and when he had recovered he had been astonished to find himself lying comfortably in the healing chambers, surrounded by crystals and with calming music playing softly in the background.

Haltingly he told his companions what he had seen and they had listened, horrified. The king had been told – but he refused to believe it and demanded a second scrying.

The second had revealed even worse devastation and the fact that this was not an event from the distant future, but was imminent, to he brought about by a series of circumstances already in train.

The king took this reading to be part of the high priest's personal and malevolent plot to unseat him by calling his way of doing things into question. He demanded that there should be a third scrying and left My-or in no doubt that if he persisted with this doom-and-gloom prognosis he would forfeit his life.

So far the prophecy had been kept from the people and only the inner council knew about it. Half of them believed with the king that it was some nefarious scheme of the high priest's. Of the others some thought he had been mistaken or was talking about the distant future. When they looked around at their beautiful and orderly world they could not imagine that it would ever he any different. Only a few, his closest friends, knew that he would not lie and that there was no oracle more reliable. They talked about it in private and deep into the night, analysing what the circumstances could be that would bring it about, knowing that certain extraordinary technological advances recently made might well put the finishing touches to a trend that they had always felt was leading towards disaster. Why was there a need for such horrific and destructive weapons?

Even the ancient crystal-lore that had helped to raise the level of their civilization above all others, was lately being abused. There was a time when crystals were used only for healing, for meditation, for communication with the Higher Self, for life-enhancement. Now their energy was being harnessed to machines to spy on others, to torture and punish, to stimulate brainwaves beyond the bounds of safety and common sense. Many who had had crystal implants in their brains had started as geniuses and ended as morons. The healing chambers could not cope with the flow of the insane who had sought artificial rather than natural intelligence. Special asylums had been opened for them, and whoever entered one of those buildings might as well abandon any hope of ever leaving.

My-or was very conscious of the safety rules devised by his predecessors and never overstepped them. But others were not so conscientious. Experiments on animals and on humans, genetic engineering, implantation of foreign elements, removal of memories by laser beams, insertion of learning in brain cells by microchip – even complete reconstructions of body and mind in an attempt to do away with death – all done with no thought for the imbalances that were being created, the dangers that were being ignored.

As he walked up the obsidian steps for the third time in as many days he thought back to the time before he noticed that things were beginning to go terribly wrong. He remembered in his youth learning the first easy steps of crystal healing. The quiet afternoons in the healing chambers, sitting with patients, placing the various configurations of crystals around them, holding the generator crystal in his hand, feeling its power for the first time, touching the tips of the crystals around the patient as though he held a taper and was lighting a series of candles. There had been time then to listen to the patient's story and choose the crystals carefully. Not like now when everything was done in such a rush. The young medics now were given lists of crystals for ailments and dispensed them automatically without adjustment to the particular soul and psyche of the patient.

He remembered the pleasure of learning about the colour rays. First there was the deep-throated chant that seemed to reverberate throughout the body, bringing all the disparate elements into alignment, giving the sense of readiness, awareness, peace. Then there was the placing of the crystals – carefully, meditatively, each colour chosen to draw down a particular ray for the particular healing. Then came the touching with the hands – the hands implanted with a whole range of etheric crystals. Finally there was the call for God's Light to enter and make whole, regenerate and heal. He hardly thought about it now. It had become instinct to use green for healing emotional imbalance, pink to clear the aura of impurities, deep blue to bring harmony and balance between the different kinds of truth that might be causing conflict within the patient (Mind, Body, and Expressive). Yellow was to clear the mind preparatory to accepting teaching. Red to strengthen vitality and clear the body of impurities. Deep violet to remove negative energies and to protect the being from possession by other beings or taking in too many harmful influences from outside.

He remembered the strongroom where the "seed" crystals were kept, those special, perfect, double-ended crystals implanted on the earth by the Ancient Ones from the destroyed planet of Atlantis – containing so much knowledge that only the highest of initiates dared use them. He remembered his first application of one of them to his third eye and the powerful visions he had received. He remembered also one of his companions fainting and refusing ever to have anything to do with them again, while another was so excited by them he overdid the exposure and became completely changed in personality. He was now the chief counsellor of the king and more than anyone responsible for the huge and lethal weapons programme in preparation.

How impatient some people are, My-or thought. The knowledge of the "seed" crystals could be good and valuable if learned at the right pace and implemented with wisdom and caution. It was meant to enlighten people about the nature of the universe, not enslave them and fill their lives with terror and despair.

Was this how the planet had been destroyed, My-or wondered. Had the original Atlanteans learned nothing from experience that they passed on their dangerous knowledge to people as imperfect as themselves? "A pity they didn't leave it all on their exploding world and come as simple colonists to ours, prepared to start again and this time take a different route. What do we need with all these vast constructions reaching to the sky, these complex computers and elaborate defences against a neighbour as frightened of us as we are of him? We have lost touch with the earth and with our Higher Selves. We seek only domination and power. Well, domination and power we will have – but not in the way we envisaged it!"

My-or wondered if it were not possible somehow to get rid of the knowledge his people were misusing. It was said that there were four great centres on the earth of extraordinary and concentrated energy: one in the Himalayas, one in the mountains of Arizona, one in the mountains of New Zealand, and the last in the earth beneath the Great Pyramid of Egypt. If only the seed crystals could be taken there and buried deep, either to be wiped clean of their imprinting by the energies present there or, if this was not possible, to lie hidden until we were morally more advanced and capable of using our knowledge without destroying ourselves and our environment.

My-or reached the top step.

He shut his eyes and prayed that he would see only the truth in the crystal bowl – only true visions.

"If it is possible," he murmured, "divert the consequences of our actions from us – forgive us – and let us start again..."

He stared unblinking into the luminous water.

In his mind the pictures began to form and he could not stop them. He knew that they had destroyed the balance of Nature – and it would be restored by force by a power greater than themselves.

He heard a cry from behind him.

He was not the only one who saw that the surface of the water was rippling, or felt the floor beneath him trembling. He looked up, dazed by being pulled back so sharply and suddenly from a vision. The faces of his companions were ashen.

He raised his hands and touched his fingertips together in a pyramid above his head. He spoke the words of the Master. He closed the scrying.

The tremor had passed and it was almost as though it had never been.

His execution by the king for false divination and spreading fear among the people only just preceded the implementation of all he'd seen.

As he died the earth split open.

The sea rose up.

Atlantis the island continent, like Atlantis the planet, was no more.

Some few had fled before the cataclysm, following their intuitions, believing the rumours. Their ships washed up on the shores of Ireland, Spain, and Africa, their people becoming wanderers and teachers, some thought to be madmen and stoned to death, others honoured and worshipped almost as gods.

Some say the great priest-magicians of the world are descended from these few – and that the great revival of crystal-lore today is due almost entirely to the reincarnation of that group of ten who stood with My-or when he foresaw the destruction of Atlantis all those millennia ago.

Only time will tell if the Atlanteans have learned their lesson and will save us from ourselves before it is too late.

Comment

The legend of Atlantis, the lost continent, has haunted us for a long time. Plato first mentioned it in c.425 BC in connection with the claim of Critias that he had heard about it from his grandfather, who, in turn, had heard about it from Solon. Solon it seems learned about it from a priest when he was travelling in Egypt.

> *For in those days the Atlantic was navigable. There was an island opposite the strait which you call...the Pillars of Heracles, an island larger than Libya and Asia combined; from it travellers could in those days reach the other islands, and from them the whole opposite continent which surrounds what can truly be called the ocean. For the sea within the strait we are talking about is like a lake with a narrow entrance... On this island of Atlantis had arisen a powerful and remarkable dynasty of kings, who ruled the whole island, and many other islands as well and parts of the continent; in addition it controlled, within the strait, Libya up to the borders of Egypt and Europe as far as Tyrrhenia.*
>
> *...At a later time there were earthquakes and floods of extraordinary violence, and in a single dreadful day and night...the island of Atlantis was...swallowed up by the sea and vanished.*

Some authorities claim that the story of Atlantis was actually a distant memory of the destruction of the great Minoan civilization of Crete in the fifteenth century BC – but Plato made a specific distinction between the sea within the straits of Gibraltar and the real ocean beyond. Most people believe that if there was an Atlantis it was in the Atlantic.

The legend of a great civilization in the past, a golden age, for which we yearn – yet from which we have been banished because we proved not to be worthy of it – is a very potent and enduring one. It expresses our faith in our potential and our disappointment in our reality.

Many legends face two ways like the old Janus god of the Romans. They face backwards in time so that the wisdom of our ancestors may nourish us, but they are also prophetic and face to the future. Because we have discovered that everything has vibrations and responds to vibration, the tale of Orpheus and his music charming the beasts, the plants, and even the rocks does not seem so far-fetched as it once did. Does this myth point "backwards' to a time when man had this knowledge, as well as "forward" to our own time when we have rediscovered it? Similarly, because we live in an age when nuclear energy has become at once the servant of man and his master, does the legend of Prometheus stealing fire from the sun take on new meaning? Was the fire Prometheus stole from the sun the fire of nuclear holocaust, the violent energy of fission, rather than the ordinary hearth fire we had originally supposed? Does not the punishment Prometheus has to endure, chained to a rock forever while vultures gnaw at his liver, sound like man's present predicament, bound in agony to the terrible secret he has learned?

Who knows but that the story of Atlantis works the same way. For some it is the history of a civilization that actually existed in the distant past, a high point in human achievement that turned to nightmare when man began to use his intelligence for domination and destruction instead of for development and creation. But what if it is a prophecy, and the intimations gifted psychics are picking up are not "far memory" at all, but prophetic warnings? The Atlantis of the future looms over us with its mighty technological marvels and its brilliant mastery of mind over matter. Will we recognize the danger in time, and develop the potential of our hearts and of our spirits as diligently as we develop our minds? No one alive today can be unaware that since Hiroshima we are in a position to destroy our entire civilization, if not our entire planet.

I have included Atlantis among the crystal legends because there is a strong belief among many of the current practitioners of crystal healing that they once lived in Atlantis and learned their craft there. Frank Alper's books in particular stress the importance of the use of crystals for more or less everything in Atlantis and give elaborate and detailed instructions. He would not call his books "legend" but history – history given to him by an ancient dead Atlantean channelling through him. It is he who claims that the earth Atlanteans came originally from another planet. Plato's "god" Poseidon?

The controversy of whether Atlantis really existed as an ancient and advanced civilization in the middle of the Atlantic ocean and subsequently sank beneath the waves goes on, some trying to point to geological evidence such as the ridge of volcanic material that runs down the centre of the ocean with a few outliers still visible (the Canaries and the Azores). Others claim that it was the first "science fiction" story, invented by Plato to make a certain point, and having no basis in fact.

Observing the rise and fall of all civilizations in the world, I see no reason why there should not have been great civilizations before us that have disappeared without trace. Too many odd and unexplained bits and pieces have been unearthed by archaeologists (from ancient rock-crystal lenses to rudimentary electrical batteries) for me to believe that we have an absolute picture of how it was in the very distant past. One can write a convincing and impressive PhD thesis on something one day and win any number of accolades from one's peers, only to be proved totally wrong by another, equally respected and meticulous scholar the next. I can even believe that there are other inhabited worlds besides our own which *could* once have visited the earth and left their trace.

The legend of Atlantis may well have sprung from a real incident in the earth's long history, but have grown beyond its origins, each generation of storytellers adding to it what its own generation needs to hear.

I find one of the most interesting phenomena connected with it is that so many people alive today are convinced that they were alive in Atlantis, or are being used as vehicles for Atlantean souls to communicate with the present generation. Is it because we are approaching the same crisis point and they genuinely exist in both spirit and reincarnation form and are trying to save us, or is it because, in approaching a dangerous crisis point, we produce desperate fantasies to help us against the terror and despair?

The incidence of channelling these days is growing alarmingly. Ancient Egyptians, American Indians, and Atlanteans are all having their say. I know a publisher who receives so many manuscripts purporting to be the work of spirits from the dead channelled through authors, some of them wise and good, but others absolute rubbish, that he has taken to wearing a button on which are the words: "Just because I'm dead doesn't mean I'm not stupid." Some mediums cynically make fortunes out of gullible people, while others offer us genuine wisdom from their spirit guides.

In a sense this channelling has always existed and still exists around the world – more frequently among the less technologically advanced peoples, those still in touch with the earth and the sky, and their own deeper natures. The novelty of it for us is only because we have been through a period when any belief in the supernatural and paranormal was jeered at and drilled out of us by people who thought scientific reality was the only reality there was. I visited the Laurentian Library in Florence a few years ago and, sitting at the very desk once used by Galileo and Leonardo da Vinci, I wrote the following:

In this honey light
scholars hatched
the new world from the old...
dared heretic's fire
to bring us the machine.
Now that all the dark corners
are clear of demons
and the sky swept bare of angels
I wonder
if they did not turn one page too many
or perhaps
write one too few.

Now that we are more and more coming to realize how limited and limiting, and in fact how outright dangerous, a materialistic only view of reality is, we are rushing back to the old beliefs, often too indiscriminately.

I included Alper's channelled book about Atlantis among my research for the legend of Atlantis because, whatever the truth of channelling is, one thing is certain: if the medium is sincere and honest, the teaching comes at least from that deep level of consciousness that yields us the precious ore of myth and legend which express the depths and heights of the human soul.

Sources

The Dialogues of Plato: Timaeus and Critias, translated by Desmond Lee (Penguin Classics, 1971): Timaeus, p. 37, Critias, p. 131, Appendix p. 146...

Ignatius Donnelly, *Atlantis: The Antediluvian World* (Harper & Bros. New York and London, 1882).

Exploring Atlantis, related through the soul of Rev Dr Frank Alper, 3 vols (Coleman Publishing, New York, 1982).

It is estimated that 5,000 books have been written on Atlantis. I have dipped into many – but the above mentioned I have consulted in more detail.

The actual story I tell above is a concoction from the tradition and is not told anywhere else exactly as I've told it here.

Two: The Crystal in the Bermuda Triangle

It seems Edgar Cayce, the famous psychic and healer of Virginia Beach, Florida, predicted that Atlantis would be discovered in 1968. In a series of explorations that began in 1968 Dr Ray Brown, a professional diver, discovered what he was convinced was an underwater Atlantean city in the area popularly called The Bermuda Triangle – an area where there seem to have been an extraordinary number of mysterious happenings this century.

Not far from Bimini he and his crew were searching for sunken Spanish galleons in the hope of finding treasure. Immensely strong magnetic readings were registered in the area. Nothing was found on that occasion, but Ray Brown was not satisfied and returned with a fresh crew. This time an accident occurred and Dr Brown experienced death. He describes feeling shock at the blow to his head from the propeller of a fishing boat, followed by a deep sense of relaxation and peace. He felt himself expanding until he not only encompassed the whole world sphere, but the universe as well.

He was dragged out of the water and pronounced dead. Suddenly he felt the life-force returning and jerked as though experiencing an electric shock.

Two weeks later he set off for the same area with four new divers. They were caught up in an enormously powerful tropical storm – a storm which not only damaged their boat but stirred up the sand on the sea bed. It was thus that they found the remains of a huge underwater city. Excitedly they explored it. At one point Brown, who was separated from the others, looked up and was dazzled by the beams of sunlight breaking through the water on to a gigantic pyramid apparently made of highly polished stone – so highly polished indeed that it resembled a mirror. On closer examination he found it was made of a blue stone that resembled lapis lazuli. He swam round and round it in amazement and on the third pass noticed an opening and swam through it. He found himself in a rectangular chamber with a peaked ceiling (rather like the chamber in the Pyramid of Kephren at Giza, Egypt, I assume). From this ceiling "a two inch diameter gold-coloured metallic rod hung straight downward, and beneath it was a pedestal, on which were metallic hands directed upward. In their grasp rested a perfectly formed crystal sphere. Around the pedestal were seven very large stone chairs." Brown's air supply was running out and he knew he had very little time. He tried to dislodge the golden rod but could not. He managed, however, to take possession of the crystal sphere. It seemed to him at that moment he felt an ominous presence in the chamber and heard a voice telling him to leave and never return.

He hurried back to the surface with his prize and, according to the article I read, has it still. It has tremendous energy. Dr Brown has become a healer and uses the crystal in his work. Heeding the warning he never returned to the place where he had found it, but sadly, the four divers who were with him did. All four were drowned. Brown says that no more tragic and mysterious disappearances have occurred in the Bermuda Triangle since the removal of the crystal.

Comment

So many experiences connected with the Bermuda Triangle and Atlantis are told these days that one does not know what to believe, or rather, on what level they are to be accepted as reality.

All this may well have happened – literally – and Dr Brown may indeed have a crystal in his possession that came from ancient Atlantis. But whether it did or not – whether Dr Brown was suffering from delusions caused by lack of oxygen or not –

the story he tells is rich in mythological significance and as such has a reality we would do well to accept.

He is swimming in the ocean of consciousness. He is dazzled by blinding light (like Saul on the way to Damascus). He sees a pyramid the shape of which, as the ancient Egyptians very well knew, draws one's awareness away from the "foursquare" world and points it towards the heavens. The pyramid is blue like lapis lazuli – the most sacred stone of the ancient Egyptians, brought all the way from the Afghan mountains and used in their sacred images for the eyes of the gods. It is shining like a mirror – the mirror in which one faces oneself – one's Self. He swims round three times – the classic number of initiation. He enters through darkness into the light interior of a sacred space. The gold bar from the ceiling is conducting the energy from the highest source of spirit to the earth, where the transformer, the crystal sphere, is waiting to receive it.

The neophyte takes the crystal. He has won it, if you like, by a long process of preparation: his vision in the "death" state; his courage in choosing to dive again after his accident; his persistence...

Note that the process started by his looking for treasure in the worldly sense, and ended with his finding treasure in the spiritual sense: the capacity to heal.

Seven chairs are around the crystal. Seven Adepts or Masters must have sat there in the ancient days transmitting the energy to the world. Seven is a number redolent with mythic power. That they sat in chairs suggests that they were in a relaxed state of meditation. They were not frantically working knobs and dials and pushing buttons. The energy was passing through their bodies and in the process becoming safer for humans to use. Brown himself uses the crystal with the energy of his own body, and so the energy transmitted is limited to what his own body can contain and pass on. If he had succeeded in taking away with him the whole Atlantean apparatus without the control of the seven Magi, who knows how much damage he might have done.

Like all sacred knowledge it is guarded against misuse. Those who are not ready for it may not have it. He is warned not to return, and those who do are drowned.

Source

A journal called *Spirals* edited by Vivienne Verdon-Roe, 1978. Report on a talk by Dr Ray Brown given at the Clearlight Foundation Conference, December 1977.

Epilogue

In the Introduction I mentioned briefly that there has recently been a tremendous upsurge of interest in crystal lore – an interest that has always been present, but has never before been acknowledged so openly and so enthusiastically.

In the last few years there have been a plethora of books about the practical uses of crystals in the New Age – *our age* – the Age of Aquarius – the age in which we are threatened with planetary extinction either by violent nuclear explosion or by the slow suffocation of pollution. Seeking anxiously for some kind of healing for the earth and the body and the soul that does not bring with it side-effects worse than the disease, many people have found their way to the crystal stalls at fairs and festivals, to workshops and lectures and courses, and, above all, to books about crystals. On my shelves alone I have such books as *The Crystal Connection: A Guidebook for Personal and Planetary Ascension* by Randall N. and Vicki V. Baer; *Crystal Enlightenment: The Transforming Properties of" Crystals and Healing Stones*, and *Crystal Healing: The Therapeutic Application of" Crystals and Stones*, both by Katrina Raphaell; *The Curious Lore of Precious Stones* by G. F. Kunz; *Cosmic Crystals: Crystal Consciousness and the New Age* by R. Bonewitz. And these I know are only a few of those recently published. The titles of some of the others picked at random from the lists of reputable publishers will give you some idea of what is being claimed for crystals these days: *The Crystal Oracle*; *Crystal Energy: Put the Power in the Palm of Your Hand*; *The Cosmic Crystal Spiral*; *Crystal Therapeutics*; *Crystal Power*; *Clearing Crystal Consciousness*; *The Crystal Sourcebook*; *The Crystal Handbook*; *Crystal Clear: How to Use the Earth's Energy to Vitalize Your Body, Mind and Spirit*; *Stone Power*; *Crystal Healing*; *Six Lessons in Crystal Gazing*; *Crystal Vision through Crystal Gazing*; *The Magic of Precious Stones*; *Healing with Crystals and*

Gemstones; *Gem Elixirs and Vibrational Healing*; *Windows of Light: Quartz Crystals and Self-Transformation*; *The Complete Crystal Guidebook: A Practical Path to Self-development, Empowerment and Healing.*

Weekend courses are available on how to open your "third eye" with crystals, on how you can learn to love your neighbour and yourself with crystals, on how you can meditate and prophesy, gain confidence, and heal with crystals.

Scientists use quartz crystals for accuracy in wristwatches and stopwatches, in clocks and telephones and computers, in radios, televisions and washing machines. The space programme would not have got off the ground without crystal technology. The atomic structure of quartz allows it "to precisely regulate electrical circuits vibrating at millions of cycles per second", explains Bruce Hathaway in his article, "Circuitry Wizards and New Agers Alike Can Get Good Vibes from Quartz" in *The Smithsonian*.

The scientists do not always agree with the claims of the psychics as to what rock crystals can do, but it is possible that there is more to crystal healing than the placebo effect. Richard Gerber, author of *Vibrational Medicine* writes:

> *We know from Einsteinian theory that all matter is basically energy. So the body is actually a complex system of energy fields. Quartz crystals apparently produce a subtle energy field that escapes measurement by traditional electro-magnetic devices, but is nonetheless capable of influencing biological organisms.*

It may well be that the ancient people who used quartz crystals for healing and exploration of the spirit planes, who incorporated them as dynamic and potent symbols in their legends and myths, instinctively knew something about crystals that it has taken the scientists with their meticulous and laborious methods a long time to confirm.

We still have a long way to go before we can satisfactorily explain why crystals do seem to work on the psyche. I personally believe it is a combination of the energy in ourselves responding to the subtle vibrational energy in the crystal, and the powerful accumulated psychological effect of thousands of years of conditioning through symbol and metaphor in myth and legend.

If we are talking about physical vibrational energy alone we cannot say, as some lecturers in crystal healing workshops do, that if we haven't got a particular crystal any other of that same colour will do. But if we are talking about symbol and metaphor, the crystal we mention takes its meaning from the context. That is why it is possible to have crystals and precious stones in one legend representing worldly wealth and, in another, spiritual riches in direct contrast to worldly wealth.

Crystal lore is part of a very ancient and very profound wisdom. I do not think it should be treated lightly. It worries me that gullible people rush off and buy, say, a rose quartz necklace convinced that within a very short while of their hanging it around their necks they will be healed of whatever ails them. The calming and healing effect of a beautiful rose quartz necklace will be wasted if the wearer is not prepared to respond to it by changing something in his or her way of thinking to remove the cause of the disease. In other words, the rose quartz by itself can do very little – but it can help you relax into a frame of mind in which you can see yourself more clearly and consequently start the process of self-healing.

It seems to me that the lists which are given out sometimes at crystal healing workshops and training sessions, and in crystal healing books, should be treated with caution. Each one will tell you a different thing – some compatible with another list, some not. For instance, one will tell you moonstone reduces excess water in tissue, another that it cures pelvic disorders; one that lapis lazuli encourages the fidelity of lovers, another that it cures tonsillitis; one that green aventurine normalizes blood pressure, eases migraine and neuralgia, another that it alleviates psychosomatic illness; one that chalcedony reduces fever, another that it stimulates bone marrow and increases production of red blood corpuscles; one that blood-stone reduces haemorrhages and nose bleeds, another that it cures tumours;

one that opal is good for the lungs, another that it is primarily for the ovaries, testicles, and pancreas.

This specific listing of the curative properties of certain crystals and precious stones seems to me a little irresponsible. I prefer the lists that are more generalized: this crystal helps one to relax, that one to be more energetic; this one helps to reduce depression, that one to increase self-control. By this we know something is expected of *us* in the healing process. *We* must gird ourselves up to tackle some problem. The crystal is there to put us in mind of what we have to do for ourselves.

So far I've mentioned only the effect of the crystal on the patient, but of course of equal importance is the effect on the healer. The healer uses the properties of the crystal – infinitesimal vibrations, colour, beauty, mythic expectation, etc. – to strengthen and encourage his or her own psychic and spiritual abilities. The crystal puts the healer in the frame of mind necessary to enable the healing energies we know exist, but which we cannot define, to flow through to the patient.

There is much talk in crystal healing circles about "programming" your crystal. Some say one should do this, others that one should not. Both parties, however, say that when you take possession of a crystal for the first time, or have been working with a crystal, you should "cleanse" it by washing it and praying over it. This is probably based on the principle behind psychometry, and, by analogy, radio and television. Vibrations and impulses undetectable to the normal human senses are imprinted on some material, amplified, and played back to us. If we are sensitive enough we can act as the amplifier for the minute vibrations and impulses that have been picked up by the crystal over its long life. Thus there are the natural vibrations or impulses of the crystal itself, plus those that it has absorbed from its environment. We have to be careful therefore that we do not "tune in" to something that is harmful.

Katrina Raphaell in *Crystal Enlightenment* says:

> *The art of attunement to a crystal, to oneself, to another person, or to any aspect of life, is one of the most valuable tools that can be learned. Tuning in is the ability to*

*neutralize the mind and become so still that the inner self
can perceive the truth.*

The Baers in their book *The Crystal Connection* put it in a
more intellectual way:

*The skull, then, can be seen as a solid-state crystalline
receiver that functions according to the sophisticated
principles of form energy. It is the selectively permeable
interface between what is outside and what is inside the
individual; it thereby serves to filter and focus universal
energies into brain-area specific profiles and pathways...*

There are many different ways of expressing ourselves when
we are thinking about crystals, but whatever way we choose
there is no doubt that the crystal has a greater effect on us than
we would expect if it were a purely physical object. This, as I
have already said, I believe to result from our age-old expectation learned in legend and myth... A sentence such as the
following from *The Glories of Glastonbury* by Armine le S.
Campbell, contains a multitude of meanings.

*When the divine office was completed, Our Lady, the
glorious Mother, in testimony of all [that Arthur had
witnessed] gave to the king a crystal cross...*

This is from the legend of the Glastonbury crystal cross. It
is simple and direct, but, like a pebble flung into a pool, it causes
ripples of interpretation and understanding to continue in the
mind for a long time. Because the crystal has so often been
associated with seeing or passing into another, higher reality;
because crystal carries the connotation of precious, of spiritual,
of supernatural, we are reminded that the wooden cross on which
the Christ was physically and painfully sacrificed, has been
transformed into a spiritual cross – a challenge for all of us.

Having spent so much time on the crystal legends, what have
we learned about ourselves?
Underlying nearly all the stories is the conviction that we

are not what we seem to be: there is more to us than we can possibly grasp at this point in our evolution.

Our consciousness is multi-layered. We may know things on the basic earthy level, or we may know them in the depths of our subconscious. But, more importantly, a third way of knowing is open to us. If we go through a process of initiation and training we may become capable of knowing things that are beyond what our senses and our machines (which are an extension of our senses) can tell us.

The Self operates on many different planes. We use our lesser selves to shop at the supermarket, to build a house, to gossip about our neighbours. We use our Higher Selves to explore other realities: to search for the meaning of life: to live according to God's Will and not our own. Most of us never find our Higher Selves. I think that one of the important messages the myths and legends in this book bring us is that nothing is set and static. We are not locked into what we are without any chance of escape; we are all in a process of change and it is in our power to effect that change. We choose the path we take, and it is our effort and courage that determines whether we win through to the "crystal palace" or not.

The stories also lead us to believe that not only are we ourselves more complex than we thought, but reality itself is more complex than we thought.

The Kabbalists expressed its complexity in terms of four realms or worlds reaching upward beyond our present understanding, each one below or above the other and yet each one at the same time "within" the other. They spoke of different forms of energy and different orders of being inhabiting each realm or world, each capable of affecting us in ours. They called the beings "demons", "angels", "archangels", "powers", "thrones", and all were aspiring in their different ways to rejoin the Source of their existence, the light beyond all light, the One beyond diversity.

These crystal legends drawn from all over our world, from civilizations at different stages, from different races and different religious traditions – all presuppose these different realms, these different beings, this searching, this striving upwards, this journey to the Source. Some call the archangels "gods and goddesses'; some call the angels "shining beings' or "spirits' or "fairies": some visualize them in one form, and others in another – but all assume that we physical beings of flesh and blood are not alone on earth, and that earth is not our only medium, our only home.

We are part of a tremendous drama, a multi-dimensional adventure, and if the legends do nothing else they give us a sense of this. They give us a crystal key fashioned by the imagination, to release the lesser self that has been locked up for so long in a small dark room. We turn it and walk out into the wide and wonderful world beyond – seeking our Higher Selves.

Sources

Randall N. and Vicki V. Baer, *The Crystal Connection: A Guidebook for Personal and Planetary Ascension* (Harper & Row, 1986).

Katrina Raphaell, *Crystal Enlightenment. The Transforming Properties of Crystals and Healing Stones* (Aurora Press, 1986).

——, *Crystal Healing: The Therapeutic Application of Crystals and Stones* (Aurora Press, 1987).

G. F. Kunz, *The Curious Lore of Precious Stones* (1913; republished by Dover Publications, 1971)

R. Bonewitz, *Cosmic Crystals: Crystal Consciousness and the New Age* (Turnstone Press, 1983).

Bruce Hathaway, "Circuitry Wizards and New Agers Alike Can Get Good Vibes from Quartz", *The Smithsonian*, Vol, 19, No. 8,1988.

Armine le S. Campbell, *The Glories of Glastonbury* (Sheed & Ward, 1926).

About Moyra Caldecott

Moyra Caldecott was born in Pretoria, South Africa in 1927, and moved to London in 1951. She married Oliver Caldecott and raised three children. She has degrees in English and Philosophy and an M.A. in English Literature.

Moyra Caldecott has earned a reputation as a writer who writes as vividly about the adventures and experiences to be encountered in the inner realms of the human consciousness as she does about those in the outer physical world. To Moyra, reality is multidimensional.

Please see www.moyracaldecott.co.uk for more information on Moyra and her work.

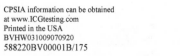